I crested the hill and looked down at the ruins in the moonlight.

The city was new.

I blinked. Nothing changed, although everything already had.

The city was alive.

People, beautiful creatures in long, colored robes, walked among pillared walkways and sat upon marble chairs. Their long hair, gold and black and red, hung like shawls over their shoulders. They moved as if in a dream, or perhaps it was because I was in a dreamlike state. For I could not say how I felt at that moment. I should have been in shock. But I didn't register what I saw as real because I no longer felt human. I moved forward, toward them, wanting to be a part of them. Yet it was as if my feet no longer touched the ground. They floated and I drifted. I could vanish into space in an instant. It was good. I was in the right place at the right time. I was coming home to a place beyond space and time. A portion of my mind left me then, and a larger part of my soul entered the void.

I stepped into the city.

I sat down on a smooth white seat.

Someone noticed me. Then another. They smiled joyfully, hopefully.

I closed my eyes and waited for them to come to me.

To serve me.

Books by Christopher Pike

BURY ME DEEP
CHAIN LETTER 2: THE ANCIENT EVIL
DIE SOFTLY
THE ETERNAL ENEMY
FALL INTO DARKNESS
FINAL FRIENDS #1: THE PARTY
FINAL FRIENDS #2: THE DANCE
FINAL FRIENDS #3: THE GRADUATION
GIMME A KISS
THE IMMORTAL
LAST ACT
MASTER OF MURDER
THE MIDNIGHT CLUB
MONSTER
REMEMBER ME
ROAD TO NOWHERE
SCAVENGER HUNT
SEE YOU LATER
SPELLBOUND
WHISPER OF DEATH
THE WICKED HEART
WITCH

Available from ARCHWAY Paperbacks

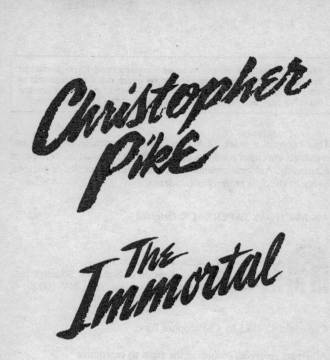

Christopher Pike

The Immortal

AN ARCHWAY PAPERBACK
Published by POCKET BOOKS
New York London Toronto Sydney Tokyo Singapore

AN ARCHWAY PAPERBACK *Original*

An Archway Paperback published by
POCKET BOOKS, a division of Simon & Schuster Inc.
1230 Avenue of the Americas, New York, NY 10020

ISBN: 0-671-74510-7

First Archway Paperback printing July 1993

10 9 8 7 6 5 4 3 2

AN ARCHWAY PAPERBACK and colophon are registered trademarks of Simon & Schuster Inc.

Cover art by Brian Kotzky

Printed in the U.S.A.

IL 14+

For Josie

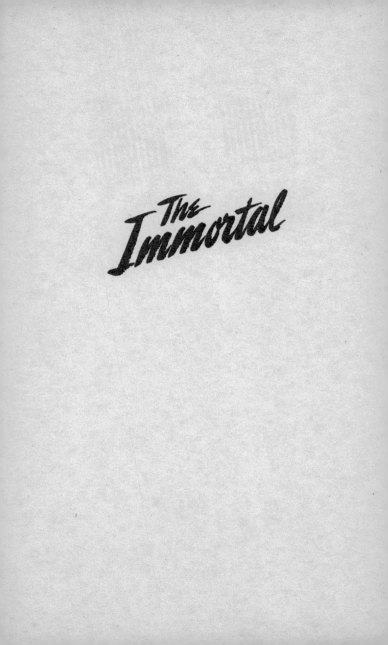

The Immortal

CHAPTER 1

MY SLEEP, AS OUR PLANE NEARED GREECE, CHANGED, BUT
I cannot say how. I would like to say that a dream, a
vision maybe, entered my unconscious state and filled
me with wonder and fear. But if this happened I
cannot remember it. I do know I *sensed* the approach
of this ancient land before I awoke. I sensed it in the
same way a child senses home, and awakens, just
before the parents pull the car into the driveway. The
stir in my sleep was familiar. I was coming home—to
a place I had never been before.

Then I heard the captain's voice announcing that
we had begun our descent. I opened my eyes and was
momentarily blinded by the morning light, a morning
that had never come so swiftly for me before. The
flight attendants had pulled up the window shades.
Yawning, stretching, I glanced over at Helen Demeter.
She was already wide awake and staring at me.

1

"Are we there yet?" I asked.

"Fifteen minutes," Helen said.

"How long have I been asleep?"

"Hours. You snore."

"I don't snore," I said quickly.

"It must have been the soul that occupies your body while you sleep that snores," Helen replied.

My mouth tasted like the last thing I had eaten before I passed out, which I think was old peanuts. I sat up straighter, heard my neck crack, and swore to myself that I must be getting old. I was stiff as a corpse.

"Do we get breakfast?" I asked.

"We just had breakfast," Helen said.

"Why didn't you wake me?"

"You didn't look hungry." Helen made a face. "You need a breath mint, Josie."

"I need a shave and a shower," I said—and my name is Josie Goodwin, and I'm a girl.

"Brush your teeth and ask a flight attendant for some orange juice. He might take pity on you. The Swiss are very polite."

We were flying Swiss Air, nonstop from L.A. to Athens. Helen and I were in coach, my father and his new babe, Sylvia—or "Silk," as she preferred to be called—up front in first class, where they could stretch their legs as far as they wished. Not only were their seats as big as ones at home, but all the champagne they wanted was on the house. I wondered if Daddy and Silk were stewed. He was drinking more

2

since he'd met his latest. My dad was a Hollywood screenwriter. He was one of the best. I didn't know what Silk was other than a pain in the ass.

"All right," I said, grabbing my carry-on bag and lurching to my feet. "Don't let anybody take my seat."

"It's not as though you can wait outside until we land," Helen called after me.

My skin was the color of wet plaster in the bathroom mirror. My blond hair was matted to my head. The veins in my eyes were the color of whiskey. And I was supposed to be pretty—really, somebody somewhere had told me that. I think it was my last boyfriend—Ralph. I had really liked him, Ralphy Boy. So had Helen, for that matter. But Ralph had moved away, and Helen and I were still friends.

I brushed my teeth and washed my face. Then I used the toilet, and that thing almost took off my butt when I flushed it. Incredible suction—I could have believed I was on the Space Shuttle. As I left the lavatory I asked a flight attendant if I could have a hit of orange juice, and he handed me a cup, made me drink it on the spot, and then told me to get in my seat. But the blue ocean, incredibly gorgeous in the first morning light, still looked a mile below us, so I rambled up to first class to see my dad.

He was sharing a joke with redheaded Silk. Outside of Hollywood, they would be an unlikely pair. Dad had balding gray hair that had failed to respond to transplants and rolls of fat that were immune to fad

3

diets—he was a battered fifty. Silk must have passed her midthirties, although she was still striving to be ready for teenage auditions. Her face was great, but hard somehow. Her firm chin may have been an implant. Her green eyes were definitely contacts. But that hair—I had to grant that Silk had hair worthy of her nickname. It flowed all the way down to her butt, which had ridden the most expensive exercise bicycles in Beverly Hills.

But in Hollywood such couples were natural. An out-of-work actress of questionable talent latching onto an out-of-work screenwriter of immense talent. Who was hoping for more? Daddy or Silky? In their own sad way they did fit together.

Sad for me.

"Hi, guys," I said, interrupting their chuckles. "Did you miss me?"

"Josie," Dad said. "We checked on you an hour ago and you were out for the count."

"You were snoring like a pig," Silk said.

I gave the sweetest smile. "At least I get it out of my system when I'm asleep," I told her.

"Jo," Dad muttered.

"Daddy," I said innocently.

But I hadn't insulted Silk, because she was too stupid to realize it. Or maybe I was wrong about that. Sometimes, when I was feeling paranoid, I wondered if Silk took in everything and simply filed it away for future reference, when her position was stronger.

"I cannot rest a moment on a plane without my blue bomber," was all Silk said.

"What the hell is that?" I asked.

"A sleeping pill," my dad said dryly. "Be grateful you slept, Josie. We're getting in early. You'll be ready for the sun and the water and we'll be in bed." He looked tired. "At least I got some writing done."

"Did you?" I asked hopefully. My father always brought his laptop computer when he traveled, but he seldom did anything more on it than write letters. He was currently doodling on a sci-fi script that he hoped would put him back on the studio executive lunch circuit. But he had writer's block—no, it was more like writer's wall, writer's mountain, writer's black hole. He hadn't had an original idea in the past year. His drinking wasn't making the situation any better. That was another reason I disliked Silk. She was under the erroneous belief that booze got the juices flowing.

My father nodded to the laptop resting on his lap and chuckled grimly. "I signed on, put in the date and time, and reread my notes."

I touched his shoulder. "The word *muse* is Greek. Maybe one of them is still hovering around the islands and will drop in and pay you a visit."

He looked up at me. "You're the only muse I need."

His compliment had a grain of truth in it. I often helped my father with story ideas. I had a knack for it.

The plane shook beneath my feet. I almost fell into Daddy and Silk's laps.

"Better sit down, dear," Silk said. "We wouldn't want you to get hurt before your vacation begins."

"I'd rather not get hurt on my vacation either," I said, like the snotty little girl I could be. Saying "See you soon," I turned and hurried back to my seat. Once there, Helen helped me fasten my seat belt.

"I didn't tell you that the Athens airport is the foulest place on the face of the Earth," Helen said. She had visited Greece the year before. Indeed, it was largely because she raved about her vacation that we were all going now. "They hate Americans with a passion. They'll spit on you the moment you get off the plane."

"But the pamphlets say the Greek people are warm and friendly," I protested.

"They're not so bad on the islands. But the airport is bizarre. Terrorists hold weekly meetings there. They sell plastique in the restrooms. You can be shot for saying, 'Hey Zeus.'"

"What?"

"'Jesus.' That's 'Hey Zeus' in Spanish. Plus the food is lousy," she added.

"Well, we won't be there long."

"We have to take a cab to another airport to catch our plane to Mykonos," Helen continued. "The cab drivers hate Americans. If you don't tip them enough they drive you back to Athens Airport and tell the people there that they didn't spit on you enough."

"You are exaggerating a tiny bit. I can tell."

Helen shook her head. "It is all very true." She

returned to her book—a travel guide to Mykonos and Delos. Like she was the one who needed to read it and not me. The plane shook some more. Over the speakers the captain said that we would be on the ground in three minutes and that the flight attendants should sit down.

"Tell me more about the nude beaches on Mykonos," I said.

Helen lit up. She was pretty when she smiled. Her hair was brown, a no-nonsense short cut, her small nose cute, something to squeeze if you were into such things. She was slight—two inches shorter than my five five—but not bony. I thought she was pretty, but even though I had known her forever, I didn't know what *she* thought. She had a talent for many things: singing, dancing, homework, art. Yet I got asked out more often, even though all I could do was help my dad with his stories.

When Helen wasn't smiling, she looked like she wasn't happy. But she would laugh when I told her that, and I would be reassured.

"The nude beaches are combined with several of the regular beaches," Helen said. "Not everyone is naked—maybe half. But few women wear tops." Helen paused. "Are you going to wear your top?"

"When my dad's around, yeah," I said. "But I'll take it off if he's not there. I'm not that shy. But I don't think I want to go totally nude. Are you going to?"

Helen hesitated. "If you don't, I won't."

"Are there a lot of gorgeous guys?"

"You mean, are there a lot of gorgeous body parts?"

"Yeah." I laughed. "Certain body parts?"

Helen nodded. "Yeah."

I rubbed my hands together. "I love vacations."

I was not a virgin, nor were Helen and Ralphy Boy. Oh, I say that so flippantly. It was not a kinky threesome—at least, not in one time frame. But Ralph Frost would certainly remember Josie Goodwin and Helen Demeter in the years to come—although maybe not in that order, since he'd gone out with Helen first. But I can honestly say I didn't steal Ralph from Helen. He had broken up with her before he asked me out. Of course, I could have said no. That's what friends are for, I know, to say no when it matters, as often as they say yes. But I didn't, then or later, when Ralph worked his seductive charm on me and we did it on the floor of his bedroom beside his huge aquarium and his bug-eyed fish. Nowadays it was hard for me to think of sex without remembering those fish. Helen, I suppose, must have the same problem.

Anyway, I think I broke Helen's heart a little for being with Ralph, and I was sorry for that. It was kind of a relief when Ralph moved away. Yet I didn't understand why he had never written to me—not a single letter, not even a card. I really did care for him. Oh well, I tried to console myself, Helen mattered more.

A few minutes later the plane landed smoothly, and when it came to a halt everyone jumped up at once as if they were going to be the first off. Helen and I were patient. I stacked my books back in my carry-on bag. I was currently into courtroom thrillers and was thinking of becoming a lawyer. Helen and I had graduated from high school a month earlier, in June. But with that thought I was being practical, because what I really wanted to be was a screenwriter like my father. The problem was, even though I was wonderful at thinking up stories, I didn't have the discipline to sit down and write anything. I couldn't even complete a letter. I wondered if Ralph hadn't written because I had never written to him.

Eventually we got off the plane. Customs was a joke. They didn't even look at our passports—just saw that we were Americans and waved us through. No one even glanced at our bags. And Helen had lectured us on how strict they were.

The airport was hot and sweaty and crowded. We each changed some money. I had my own; it wasn't courtesy of my dad. I worked with a caterer twenty hours a week. The official currency of Greece was the drachma. Right then we got a hundred and sixty of them for a dollar. I changed two hundred U.S. dollars, and with the wad they handed me in return I felt rich. Helen was anxious to get us over to the other airport to make our connection to Mykonos. Helen was always neurotic about time.

No one spit on us, but no one smiled either. We left the airport, our bags piled in a couple of rental carts, and got in a long line to catch a cab. The sun was intense and I began to perspire. The buildings in the vicinity were dirty. I couldn't complain—I was from L.A.

"It's cooler on Mykonos," Helen said as I wiped my forehead.

"That's good," I said. "How long is the flight there?"

"A half hour," Helen said.

"Will there be someone to meet us at the airport?" Silk asked. She had dressed up for the trip—always a mistake. Her purple dress and coat were close to being ruined. She had brought more bags than the rest of us combined. Helen and I were dressed casually in khaki shorts. Dad had on a pair of pants he should have thrown out the year before. He had to unbutton them to sit down.

"It's questionable," he said.

"Oh, Bill, didn't you make sure?" Silk asked, a whiny tone to her voice. Silk had a habit of whining when she was tired and if she didn't get her daily nap, which was supposed to be at about five o'clock. I hated whiners.

"I faxed the people at the hotel a number of times, honey," Dad said. "They said they'd do what they could. We can always catch a cab."

"The cab drivers on Mykonos are all crazy," Helen told Silk. "They hate redheads with a passion. They think they're witches."

"Oh, dear," Silk said.

We finally got a cab. The driver drove like a madman. I supposed I would have done the same if I had to wait in line at the airport several times a day—it would have driven me nuts. He took us straight to Olympic Airlines. At the terminal I had to help with Silk's luggage—we all had to. I handled her bag roughly; it felt as if it was stuffed with back issues of *Cosmopolitan,* maybe an X-rated video or two. We groped our way inside, out of the heat and into an oven, and still no one spat on us. Helen looked disappointed when I pointed that fact out to her.

The flight to Mykonos was in forty minutes. I amused myself by sitting on the floor—all the seats were taken—and reading my latest thriller. The hero was about to find out that the woman he was defending had not only actually committed the murder but had cheated on the bar exam as well when the two of them had taken it twenty years earlier. Spicy stuff. I glanced over at my father as he typed in a few words on his laptop and gave him a wink. He smiled—he knew he wasn't going to write more than a useless sentence or two in a crowded airport.

At last we were on the plane, a two-engine prop job that I hoped had been built in the U.S. Inside, before takeoff, it was a thousand degrees, and it warmed my heart to see Silk on the verge of passing out. But the air-conditioning came on once we were in the air. I sat in the back of the plane beside Helen. She peered out the window.

"I have always dreamed of renting a sailboat and sailing from island to island," she said, almost with a sigh. "Wouldn't that be heaven?"

"It does sound wonderful," I said. "Maybe we can do it when we get older—and learn to sail."

"Sailing around these islands is not always that easy. There's a wind that comes up around Mykonos called the *meltémi.* One second the water is flat and calm and the next it's churning. The *meltémi* will probably kick in a time or two while we're here."

Half an hour later we were at Mykonos. We had to walk from the plane to the terminal. The airport was small; there were no pushing crowds. The surrounding terrain was rocky, hilly—what tourists thought all Greek islands were. Yet even though it was arid, it was beautiful. I liked it immediately. Athens had not been as horrible as Helen had described, but there had been a certain heaviness to the place. Mykonos was the opposite. There was a feeling of life in the air, of fun, of adventure. Indeed, I suddenly felt as if I had reached an important crossroads in my life. I knew this would be a trip to remember for a long time.

There was a gentleman waiting for us—Mr. Ghris Politopulos. At first I assumed he was a hired hand at the hotel where we were staying, but he was both the owner and the manager of the place. His face was fascinating, thick-lipped with a warm smile and the palest, coldest blue eyes I had ever seen—one of which was lazy, rolling this way and that as he scanned our luggage.

"Welcome to Mykonos," he said in heavily accented English. "You will love it here. But this"—he gestured to our bags—"you don't need so many clothes here. Mykonos is always warm this time of year."

"I have many of your father's things in my bags," Silk said to us, annoyed at the hired help questioning what she'd brought.

"Do our rooms have ocean views?" Helen asked Mr. Politopulos.

"One of the rooms does," he replied.

Helen flashed a glance my way and we shrugged in unison. We both knew which room would be ours, and that was fine. Helen's parents had paid for her plane ticket, but my father was shouldering the hotel bills. Helen's trip was a present from my father to me.

We boarded Mr. Politopulos's van and headed for the hotel. Mykonos was not big, only ten miles across, and soon we were bouncing our way along the outskirts of Hora—the main city on the island. Mr. Politopulos explained the colorful history of Hora. Egyptians, Phoenicians, Cretans, and Ionians had all lived on the island in the B.C.s. Turks and an endless train of pirates had run the place later—the population would explode, then become almost extinct depending on which way the winds of war were blowing. It wasn't until the 1950s that tourism took hold and island life began to resemble what it was today. At that Mr. Politopulos laughed, saying that Mykonos was basically a big party island. He had been born on Mykonos and had lived his whole life there.

We never entered Hora, however, but turned south away from the city for the remainder of the ride to our hotel. It was only then I got my first good look at the sea, and I was in love. The water was a jewel blue the California coast would never know, the sand clean and uncluttered, lazily draped with brown bodies of enviable shape and elusive covering. Already I could see several pairs of male buns and knew I would have a crick in my neck long before the vacation was over.

Helen pointed to an island out at sea, perhaps five miles away. "That's Delos," she said. "The most sacred island in the Aegean Sea."

"Why is it so sacred?" I asked.

"Because Apollo and his sister Artemis were born there," she said.

The sun flashed in my eyes as I stared at the island. I had to close them briefly, and once more I had that same sense of coming home that I had had on the plane. I felt I had been to this place before.

"I want to go there soon," I whispered.

"We'll go there tomorrow," Helen said, watching me.

Our hotel was simple, with whitewashed walls built to withstand the heat and sun. It was well situated beside a beach, but close enough to town so that we could walk in at night for the party life. Mr. Politopulos checked us in and showed us our rooms, helping us with our bags. Dad and Silk's suite was spacious and on the second story overlooking the surf. Mr. Politopulos warned us to watch the doors and windows when the wind was blowing.

"A man last week got struck on the head by a

window and had to be taken to the hospital for stitches," he said. "The *meltémi*—it blows fiercely when the gods are in the mood."

"The gods," I muttered. "Does anyone in Greece worship the ancient deities?"

Mr. Politopulos smiled, his lazy eye staring at my rubber sandals, his other one regarding my face. "Not worship," he said. "But many still respect them."

Our room was on the ground floor, in the back. It had a view of sorts. It overlooked a corner of the swimming pool, where, by golly, there were a lot of naked females enjoying the sun. We had narrow twin beds and a bathtub that looked as if it had been designed for a race of dwarfs. Neither of us believed we would be spending that much time in our room.

"Are you tired?" I asked Helen. Her brown eyes were bloodshot.

"A little. But if I sleep now I'll never get on the schedule here." She stowed her cheap suitcase in the corner. Her family didn't have much money, even though it seemed as if they must because their only daughter had gone to Greece twice in a year. Her parents were anxious to keep her happy—for various reasons. Of course my dad was running low on funds as well. He had to sell something soon, even if it was only a movie-of-the-week or a sitcom pilot.

"Do you want to go into town and walk around?" I asked.

"No, we can do that after the sun goes down. That's when the action starts. Let's go snorkeling, but not here. The beaches on the other side of the island are much nicer—there are Agrari and Paradise." Helen rolled her eyes. "Lots of naked bodies on those beaches."

"How do we get there?" I asked. "Can we take a bus?"

"Maybe, but we don't want to. The best way to get around is on a motorbike. We can rent them outside of town for less than fifteen bucks a day. Have you ever ridden a motorbike?"

"No, but I'm game." I had seen couples on the bikes on the way to the hotel and it looked like fun.

"You have to learn how to shift gears. No one wears a helmet here. It can be dangerous."

"If you did it, I can do it," I said.

Helen was amused at my confidence. "We'll see," she said.

We changed into fresh shorts and T-shirts and bade my father and Silk goodbye. They were already half asleep. Hora was ten minutes on foot. Walking into town along a bumpy asphalt road, we passed what looked like a worthy beach. I still couldn't get over how clear the water was. But Helen reassured me that the beach was nothing compared to what we would see on our motorbikes.

The surrounding houses were all white, dazzling in the sunlight, their balconies festooned with glorious geraniums and pots of basil. Closer to the city, the houses grew thicker together, and I could see that one facade blended into the next, with narrow flagstone alleys winding between them. Helen stopped at a bike shop at the edge of this wonderful town.

She was familiar with the bikes, and I suspected she had used the place on her previous trip. A pleasant young Greek woman with spotty English helped us pick out bikes—two new Hondas. She demonstrated how to shift gears, kicking successively down with the left foot. It didn't look hard, but Helen warned me that I would need practice to get the hang of it.

"Wait till you're going uphill," she said. "Then you'll have fun."

Helen's prophecy came to rapid fruition. Our bikes were low on fuel, the Greek woman warned us. We had to go straight to the gas station, and by luck the place was straight up the hill from the shop. I got the bike going well enough and was out on the road, but I quickly lost speed as the incline steepened. Helen was in front of me, pulling away, as cars and other motorbikes roared past me. I thought I was in first gear, the best one for a steep hill, but I must have been in second. I kicked the gear lever, and still I continued to slow down. The bike slowed to the point that it was in danger of falling over. Then it stalled. I coasted over to the side and dug my sandals into the asphalt. The bike was trying to roll back down the hill.

"Damn," I said.

The scooters had kick starters. I fiddled with the gears before giving it a kick and discovered I had been in third gear. Using the heel of my left foot—the front of the foot upped the gears, the heel lowered them—I ground myself back to what I hoped was neutral and then, with my right foot, gave the starter pedal a good swipe. Apparently I wasn't aggressive enough. Starting a bike is a real macho thing, I realized. Putting a slight sneer on my lips, as if I were James Dean, and gritting my teeth, I gave the pedal a real he-man slap. It roared to life.

I rode all the way up the hill in first gear. I was taking no chances on stalling out. Helen was waiting for me at the gas station, a smug expression on her face.

"Having trouble?" she asked.

"Not at all." I swung my leg off the bike, feeling cool.

Helen nodded to the pump. "One full tank will last us three days. I told you, this is the way to get around. Just don't crack your skull on the pavement and we'll have a blast."

We gassed up and were soon on our way to Paradise Beach. Helen had decided on that one. The road continued to rise for half a mile. Soon we were treated to a glorious view of the western side of the island. Then the city was behind us and we were in the back country—if it could be called that. The silhouettes of windmills on the hills were a reminder of days gone by. There was so much gray rock, its domain broken only by the many white chapels, raised on outcroppings so forbidding I wouldn't have wanted to approach them on a windy day. I counted eight churches in the space of a mile. I had read a bit about them in

Helen's travel book. Apparently prosperous sailors long ago were fond of erecting them before going on a dangerous sea voyage. The hope was to gain divine protection.

The road was bumpy and hilly, but I could have been a Hell's Angel in a past life. My mastery of the shifting gears came with a few minutes of experimentation. I do believe it was a look of shock on Helen's face when I came roaring by her at thirty-five miles an hour. The warm air and the brilliant sunlight were a delight on my face and bare arms. The blue coast of the other side of the island came into view. My laughter must have rung in Helen's ear as I passed her. Suddenly I realized I was on vacation and having the time of my life.

A few miles later a splintered wooden sign pointed the way to Paradise, to the right, off the main road. By this time Helen had drawn abreast, warning me not to get too cocky. Together we turned onto the gravel road that led down to the beach. I wore sunglasses, as did Helen, but the rays of the sun sparkled on the water like igniting jewels, and occasionally I had to shield my eyes. It was an odd thought to have, but it was hard to believe it was the same sun in the sky that had shone on me all my life in L.A. I remembered that in Greek mythology Apollo was associated with the sun.

We parked and locked our bikes and sauntered down to the beach. Near the sea the mass of gray rock turned to golden sand before being covered by crystal blue waters. There were no waves—who needed them? The sea was various shades of cerulean, changing color with the depth. The sand was lighter in color than the California brand, but grainier. There were beautiful people everywhere, and only half of them had bathing suits on. I liked to look—who doesn't? And I had never before had so many young men to stare at. I can honestly say, without a shred of shame, that I didn't miss Ralphy Boy one bit right then.

"We should have grown up here," Helen said.

"We should move here," I replied. "Who needs college."

"You can see why I wanted to come back."

"I can't see why you left."

We had towels that we'd borrowed from the hotel. We didn't have snorkeling equipment, however, or sunscreen. I had frequented the beach since school had let out and had a good tan. Indeed, I never burned, no matter how long I lay out. But Helen had a problem. It was a priority to get her fair skin firmly shielded behind sunblock, thirty or better.

We took care of the screen for Helen in a small store and were directed to a stand farther down the beach that was supposed to rent masks, fins, and snorkels. All at once Helen was not anxious to get in the water. She said she wanted a drink and pulled me toward the bar, located at the rear of the beach under a thatched roof.

"There was this guy from England who worked here last summer," she said. "He said he'd be back this summer."

"Is he the reason we're at this beach?"

"It's a nice beach."

"I understand," I said.

"His name's Tom Brine. We went out a couple of times." She added unnecessarily, "I liked him."

"Maybe he has a friend," I said hopefully. I wasn't looking for a quick vacation romance, I told myself. On the other hand I wasn't swearing off one, either, which was, I thought, the best attitude.

The bar was crowded. There was no sign of Tom. A shade subdued, Helen ordered a beer, and I did likewise, after a moment's hesitation to note that they weren't asking for ID. I didn't drink a lot, even at parties, because I invariably woke up with a headache. But I had to watch Helen when it came to booze. She had a tendency to do things to excess. We turned our backs to the bar and sipped our beers, enjoying the view.

"He could be here this summer but taking the day off," I ventured.

"I didn't expect to find him," Helen said quickly, lying.

"What was he like?"

"Funny. Smart." She added, perhaps in reference to the Ralph episode, "You would have liked him."

"Was he cute?"

"Who?" a voice asked behind us.

We turned in unison and Helen's face broke into a big grin. I didn't have to ask. Tom Brine was a cutie. His face was pale, typical of many English young men.

He seemed to be scholarly in a way with alert green eyes and messy brown hair that the sun was swiftly turning the color of the sand. He was thin but in good shape and stood remarkably straight, as if at attention. I put his height at six feet, maybe an inch more. He was a couple of years older than we were.

"Tom, do you remember me?" Helen asked.

He scratched his head. "You're from America, right?"

"Yeah," Helen said, a little worried. The lifeguard on duty would have known we were from America.

"You were here last summer?" Tom continued.

"Yeah," Helen said.

Tom gave a sly smile. "You break into wicked Italian while in the heat of making passionate love?"

Helen hit him playfully. "That girl came earlier in the summer! I know you remember me. You look too happy to see me."

Tom snapped his fingers suddenly. "Melon!"

"Helen!"

"We went out once," Tom said. It seemed to come to him all at once and give him pleasure.

"Twice." Helen leaned her elbows on the bar. I hadn't seen her so excited in a long time. "You had the time of your life."

"Was I sober?" he asked.

"Most of the time," Helen said. "How have you been, Tom? Oh, this is my friend, Josie. Josie, meet Tom. He's from England."

Tom was quick to shake my hand. He gave me the once-over but was subtle about it—I only knew from his eyes. His accent was a delight. I had always thought English accents sounded cultured.

"Josie," he said. "You are definitely from California and you definitely know Italian."

"Just the naughty words," I said.

He laughed and nodded to my beer. "How's your drink keeping?"

I took a gulp from the bottle—some German brew. "Great."

"Hey, I'm here for a week," Helen said. "When do you get off work?"

"When the sun goes down," Tom said. He had been drying glasses as he spoke. He had big hands, skillful fingers. "I'd love to get together with you ladies later."

"I don't know if you could handle two of us at once," Helen said, her smile forced. "Do you have a friend for Josie? She's just getting over a heartbreaking affair."

"That I've already forgotten," I murmured. She might have been talking about Ralph, I think, or she might have simply been talking.

"There's Pascal," Tom said. "Do you remember him? Big? French?"

"I'm not sure," Helen said.

"You may not have met him," Tom said. "His English is only fair." Tom looked at me. "But the ladies all like him."

"The ladies might not have the same taste as I do," I said.

Helen and Tom narrowed down when and where they would meet. I felt hot from the ride in the sun and I was anxious to get in the water. Yet—and I am a horrible friend—I liked Tom. He seemed like a nice guy. Of course, they all do at first.

We said our goodbyes and went for snorkel equipment. Helen asked me what I thought of him.

"He's cool," I said. "I hope his friend is as nice. But big, French, and can't speak English—what are you getting me into?"

"We'll have fun," Helen assured me.

The snorkel equipment was inexpensive: the whole works for eight dollars a day. We told them we wanted it for three. Helen used her credit card this time. I had put mine down when we rented the bikes. We would figure who owed what later. Neither of us was picky about money.

The water was warm, clean, colorful—I couldn't get over how much I loved it. With our equipment on, we paddled out to a number of docked sailboats and then swam over to the jetty. I swear, we were in fifty feet of water and I could see the eyes of the fish on the bottom eating from the long grasses that grew up from the sand. There was no coral, but plenty of interesting stone. I had a fantasy as I snorkeled that I would suddenly spot a gleam of buried treasure. But it was just a dream.

The fish, of course, made me feel kind of horny.

We had been snorkeling for close to an hour when I suddenly felt a pain in my chest. It started in the center and quickly spread in a band across my ribs. The pain was frightening, but not totally unexpected. I was overdoing it. Ten months earlier, at the end of the previous summer, I'd had a bout with pericarditis, which is an inflammation of the sack surrounding the heart. It can hit with varying degrees of intensity. My illness had been particularly severe. I was hospitalized for three weeks, ten days of which I spent in intensive care. The disease hit with incredible speed and had at first mystified the doctors. By the time I was diagnosed, I was close to death. My fever was so high I lay in semiconscious slumber for days, knowing little, except that I was in pain, horrible pain every time I took a breath.

Yet after the illness I had been happy, for it seemed that by coming so close to death I had gained a new appreciation for life. The simplest things that I had taken for granted, such as walking to school in the morning or eating ice cream, now came to have special meaning for me. I had also decided to take my future more seriously and buckled down with my studies. My grades my senior year had reflected my newfound dedication. I got almost straight *A*'s.

The doctors believed I had made a full recovery, without permanent damage to my heart, but they had warned that my endurance would only return gradually. Even now, so many months later, I was aware that I was not at full strength.

The pain hit me when I was near the end of the jetty, a quarter mile out. I briefly contemplated trying to climb onto the rocks and resting, but there were waves, battering the jetty hard enough to knock me down if I tried to stand up, and the rocks were covered with moss that looked slippery. Helen was fifty yards off to my right, swimming circles around a huge yacht. I debated calling out to her but was embarrassed. I know it was foolish. Helen was my old friend. My problem was genuine. I was having trouble breathing; I was on the verge of cramping. But I hated to appear weak, particularly in front of her. The aversion had started the previous summer, after my illness.

Slowly I began to swim toward the beach. How quickly perceptions could change. Moments before the beach had looked within arm's reach. Now it was miles away. I cautioned myself to take my time, to breathe slowly and deeply. At first the strategy worked. I was halfway in and looking good. But then all at once I tired. The pain in my chest returned like a hammer pounding. The muscles in my legs knotted and stiffened. I had been saving my arms—every good snorkeler knew the arms couldn't compete with fins. Panic entered my mind. Could I actually drown in front of five hundred sunbathers, on my first day of vacation? The thought sent a shot of cold terror up my spine. I began to thrash with my arms, trying to pull myself to shore as fast as possible.

It was the worst thing I could have done. In a minute I was exhausted and gasping for air. I pulled my head out of the water and took my mouth off the snorkel—another mistake. It was easy, while snorkeling, to just relax in the water, facedown, and not even paddle at all. But all I could think of was getting to shore.

I accidentally took in a mouthful of water and

coughed. Now I was eagerly searching for help and I wouldn't have minded if it came from Saddam Hussein. But I was at the end of the beach. The sole lifeguard was in the middle, and he had plenty of naked women to look at on the shore, and I think he was asleep anyway. I didn't glance behind me, to see if Helen was nearby. I didn't want to turn away from the beach for even a second because I feared I might move a foot away from it.

I couldn't swim properly with my head out of the water, but I was too shaken to replace my snorkel and put my face back down. The pain in my chest was like the heat from a torch blowing blue flame through the lobes of my lungs. Honestly, I thought I was going to have a heart attack. The smell of the hospital came back to me then, the vapor of rubbing alcohol, the beep of the monitors in intensive care. It seemed that beep had been the first thing I heard when I had awakened from my long burning dream, a mechanical pulse in my ears, some bloodless heartthrob. *Beep, beep, beep*—you're alive, little girl. But it seemed there had been a pause—I suddenly remembered this—a short one, when the beeps had stopped, and there had been silence. . . .

I felt myself sinking.

Nothing but the silent roar of cold air blowing through a wide empty space. Yes, I remembered, the beep had definitely stopped.

"Josie!" a voice spoke in my ear.

A strong arm yanked my head up.

I blinked—I must have closed my eyes.

"God," I gasped.

It was Tom.

The shore was still a hundred yards away. Tom was swimming in place beside me. He still had his work shirt on. How he had gotten there didn't matter, not to me. His arms were around my waist, lifting my mouth and nose out of the water.

"Just relax," he said, slipping behind me, moving his arm under my arms. "Relax into me, Josie. I'll tow you in."

"I'm all right," I said, coughing.

"The hell you are."

We were in shallow water a couple of minutes later. Tom helped me remove my fins and took my mask and snorkel. He held me by the arm while I staggered onto the beach. There I collapsed on the sand, grateful for the chance to catch my breath. I was not having a heart attack. The pain in my chest began to diminish. In the space of five minutes I was almost fully recovered and terribly embarrassed. Helen came running out of the water and stopped beside Tom, staring down at me.

"What happened to you?" Helen asked.

"Nothing," I muttered.

"I think she cramped up," Tom said.

Helen was amazed. "And you came to her rescue?"

Tom shrugged. His shirt was dripping wet, along with his shorts. "I was watching the two of you from my place at the bar. I noticed Josie having trouble."

"Why didn't you call me for help?" Helen asked me.

"I got a little tired is all," I muttered. "I didn't need to be rescued."

Helen knelt by my side, taking my hand. She spoke to Tom. "Josie was in the hospital last year. It's easy for her to overdo it. She has a bad heart. She—"

"I do not have a bad heart," I interrupted angrily. My humiliation was deepening. I forced a smile and shook off Helen's hand. "Don't talk about me like I'm an invalid." I glanced up at Tom. "I'm OK, I would have been OK. But I want to thank you for your concern anyway."

Tom nodded. He understood I didn't want a big deal made of the matter. "I'd better get back to my job. They're not paying me to be a lifeguard."

Helen stood up and touched his chest. "Thank you for saving my friend, Tom," she said sweetly but seriously.

"Oh, brother," I mumbled, my eyes rolling.

"I didn't mind a nice cool dip," Tom said.

"See you tonight," Helen said. She raised up on her toes and kissed his cheek. Tom nodded and turned to leave. Helen knelt beside me once more.

"Are you really all right?" she asked.

I sat up and sighed. "Yes."

"What happened?"

"Nothing."

"Why didn't you at least act grateful to Tom for saving your life?"

"My life was not in danger!" I snapped. Then I quieted down. "I got tired is all. I don't like this being made into a big production."

Helen nodded, studying me. "You embarrass easily, Josie."

I returned her stare. "So do you, Helen." I added, "Let's not talk about this with my dad. It'll only make him worry."

"I understand," Helen said.

"Good." I got up. "Let's get out of here. Too many people are staring at me."

CHAPTER 2

THE SKY WAS ALMOST DARK WHEN I AWOKE FROM MY NAP. I was alone in my room. After returning from Paradise Beach, I had lain down in bed for a quick rest. Neither Helen nor I had intended to pass out for any length of time. We didn't want to sleep during the day and be up all night. I didn't know if Helen had managed to stay with the game plan, but when I checked my watch and discovered I had been out for four hours, I realized it might take a few days to adjust to the new time zone. My chest felt fine, no pain at all.

Dressing in blue jeans and a yellow blouse, I left the room and searched for the others. I didn't go straight to my father's room but passed through the lounge area at the front of the hotel, where there was a small bar and snack shop. There I found Silk, watching a rerun of "Gilligan's Island" and stirring a bloody

Mary. What a prize, I thought; she came all the way to Greece to watch bad TV. We had the lounge to ourselves.

"Where's my dad?" I asked.

"He's in the room, writing," Silk replied. She had on a suede purple pants outfit, too much make-up. With the approaching night it had cooled some, but it was still too warm for suede. Silk took a sip of her drink. Her gaze was easy, too accepting; it had not been her first transfusion from Mary, I realized.

"What did you do today?" I asked.

"Went for a walk on the beach."

"Did you go in the water?"

"It's too cold."

"The water is in the eighties, for godsakes."

"Don't swear," she said.

"What?"

"I said, don't swear. A girl your age should watch her mouth."

I snorted. "A girl your age should watch her liver."

Silk giggled. If it had been her first drink she would have been annoyed. "You don't like me much, do you, Josie?"

I shrugged. "What's there to like?"

Silk put her feet up on a nearby chair. "I don't know. I'm not a bad person. I'm pretty. I'm talented. I make your father happy."

"You don't bring him happiness. You bring him distraction."

"In this world the two are synonymous."

32

I sat beside her. "In *your* world the two are synonymous. My father has talent; you have schemes. You like my father for what he has, what he can do for you. Well, I have to warn you, in Hollywood sleeping with a writer is no way to break into the movies. The writer is way down on the totem pole, below the director, the producer, the studio execs, and the stars. You'll never be a star, Silk. You can't fool an entire audience. You'll never be my father's wife. You may be able to fool him for the time being, but he's smart. He has nothing in common with you."

Silk blinked at me, dazed, then belched into her drink before moving the glass to her lips. "You sound pretty sure of yourself for a bitchy little snot," she muttered.

I grabbed her drinking arm before her mouth could touch the booze. I held it hard for a moment, wanting to shake the drink onto her clothes. Silk stared at me, momentarily helpless. I saw then how pathetic her life was, living this fantasy that was so deeply entrenched that she actually rehearsed her Oscar acceptance speech each night before she went to bed. I had heard her reciting it through the wall. I let go of her arm, suddenly ashamed of myself.

"I'm sorry," I said. "We're on vacation. I shouldn't be chewing you out at a time like this."

"I heard you almost drowned," Silk said abruptly as it were pertinent to our discussion.

I got to my feet. Helen had betrayed my confidence. "I didn't 'almost' drown. I just faked it so that a handsome boy could come rescue me."

Silk nodded her approval. "I'll have to try that someday. When I learn to swim."

I found my father on the terrace off his room with his humming laptop on a table in front of him. He sat overlooking the sea. He turned to me as I approached. His door had been unlocked and I entered without knocking. The wind had risen since we arrived and was now churning the gray waves. The western sky was a gray and weary orange. I had missed the sunset by half an hour. What light remained silhouetted the island of Delos, changing it to a shadow realm out at sea. My father gestured to the chair beside him, and I sat down.

"I ran into Silk in the lounge," I said.

"How is she?" he asked.

"Feeling no pain."

He waved his hand. "She's on vacation. Let her enjoy."

"All right." I paused. "You're on vacation, too. Why don't you enjoy? You don't have to write the first day you get here." He appeared troubled at my remark. I reached over and touched his leg. "It will flow again. You'll see."

He watched the waves reflectively. "I wonder. When the stories are there, you don't know where they come from. When they stop, you don't know where they've gone. It's as if a story exists only in the moment—if you don't quickly write it down or show it to someone else, it vanishes." He sighed. "Sometimes, Josie, I feel as if I've moved out of that moment. Like I'm living in the past, a few seconds behind the times, in the shadow of them. Or else in the future, a few months from now, when I think things will be better." He shrugged again. "Whatever, I'm stuck and I don't know what to do."

"Tell me your story from the beginning," I said. "I know you've told me parts of it before, but tell me it all now."

He was reluctant. "There's nothing more shameful than telling people that you're working on a screenplay, and then having it discovered that you've worked out little more than the opening credits."

"I know that."

He smiled affectionately. "I know you know that. That's why you're the one I can talk to. All right, you know the name—*Last Contact*. It's a science-fiction thriller. It takes place five hundred years in the future. Mankind has expanded out across this portion of the galaxy and is living on hundreds of planets circling dozens of stars. They are at war with an alien race. They have been at war for two hundred years. The aliens are humanoid—I know that much—but they don't look like us. The Earth has long been destroyed when we enter the story."

"Excuse me, Dad," I interrupted. "Why are you so sure the Earth has already been destroyed?"

He shrugged. "When the story first started coming to me, I knew the Earth was finished. It was just one of those things I knew in my gut. That fact makes the war with the aliens especially bitter. There is no possibility of compromise. The aliens must be destroyed, or else mankind will be. Unfortunately, humanity is losing the war. This is the setting when we meet our main character.

"His name is David Herrick. He's an ace pilot for the System—the name I have given to the collection of human-inhabited planets. Much of the fighting in this war is carried out in small one-man spaceships. I am going on the theory that in the future our offensive weapons will be stronger than our defensive abilities. To give an example: I don't think we'll be able to 'raise shields' against the weapons that will be developed. I believe a small vehicle will be able to deliver almost as much damage to a planet as a larger one, and there will be little protection against attack. Therefore, I have thousands of one-man fighters up against the aliens rather than a few huge starships. Do you follow?"

"Yes," I said. "It's logical. Go on."

"David Herrick is one of the best pilots the System has. Although young—in his early thirties—he's been on many successful raids against the aliens. He is cunning, resourceful, and brave—all the best qualities you'd want in a hero. But one thing about these pilots—they are all marked men. Inevitably they will—if they continue to be pilots—be killed. The System trains thousands of them, and thousands of them die each year. David has lived longer than most.

"The movie starts with David being called in by his superiors. The System has captured, for the first time, an alien ship. Better than that, they have captured the two aliens who were commanding the vehicle. Through an intensive process of torture and brainwashing, they have broken one of the aliens—the female. The other one died in captivity. From the alien female, they have learned where the alien home planet is located. The world is heavily guarded, of course, but the military intelligence of the System believes that they can use the alien ship, and the alien herself, to sneak into the alien solar system, set a bomb on the home world, and escape. They feel that if they can destroy the alien home world, they will break the backbone of the enemy, and the war will be over.

"The System has chosen David to lead this expedition. It is extremely dangerous. The chance that he will be found out before he can reach the home world of the aliens is high. There is even a possibility he will be captured and tortured. But David doesn't think it's likely. He'd die before he'd allow himself to be taken prisoner. In many ways David is well suited for the mission. You see, Josie, he has recently learned his wife is leaving him for another man.

"David's wife is named Jessica. We meet her in a series of flashbacks as the movie progresses. At first the flashbacks are pleasant. We see David and Jessica going for long walks along wine-colored canals, beneath brilliant starry skies. But then we see how their marriage suffers under the strain of David's career. Each time David leaves on a mission, Jessica has to accept the fact he may not return. Jessica knows it is only a matter of time before he is killed. So her love is intense, but also painful.

"But at the start we don't know all this. We only know that David is eager to go on the mission, that he hates the aliens with a passion, and that he doesn't seem to give a damn about anything other than killing them. David's superiors take him to learn how to handle the alien ship. They also introduce him to the female they have captured. Her name is Vani. She is not pleasant to look at. She is hairless, her skull protrudes in a number of colored lobes, and she has hands that are more like talons than fingers. At the same time she has definite female characteristics. Her voice, in particular, is soothing. David hates her the moment he meets her. He anticipates using her against her own people.

"Vani has an implant in her brain that can make her experience pain in varying degrees. That is how David will control her. For example, say they come to a checkpoint while entering the alien solar system. He will need Vani to say the right things to gain him entrance. She will do exactly what he wishes without him hardly having to turn the dial on the control connected to the pain implant because she has been totally devastated by the torture she has gone through. Even though David despises her, he also sees her as a pathetic creature.

"The two take off toward the alien home world. David has aboard his ship a bomb the size of a basketball, but one that is filled with antimatter—capable of devastating a whole planet. The alien home world is far away. David has to circumvent the entire local region of the galaxy to get to it. The ship is capable of ultra light speed, but still the journey takes many months. Both of them sleep away most of the time in hibernaculums. During this time David dreams of his wife, and we see in detail how his relationship fell apart.

"When they awake they are near their goal. But they have to go through numerous checkpoints to get to the alien solar system. Here I have a couple of action sequences. We see Vani aiding David past one particular security check, only to have the aliens get suspicious. In the end David has to destroy them, which adds pressure to his mission. He is not sure if he has already blown his cover. Yet he presses forward.

"During this time, though, he gets to know Vani, and now has trouble hating her. She is pleasant, nicer than most human beings, and he talks freely with her about his troubles with his wife. She listens well. He discovers that the man the System tortured to death, the one who was with her when she was captured, was her husband. He feels bad about that but then decides it is war. He doesn't empathize with her so much that he forgets that Vani's people were the ones who destroyed the Earth. Vani does not deny this fact either.

"But there are things Vani is incapable of discussing. She will go to speak them, and a wave of pain will overcome her. It is obvious that during her torture she was conditioned not to speak of certain matters. One of these is the one-way nature of the mission David has undertaken. Yes, his is a suicide mission. He begins to figure it out anyway, even without her assistance. It makes sense. The System would want his bomb to go off the moment the ship entered the atmosphere of the alien home world. That way, if David and Vani got that far, there would be no possibility of failure.

"David reasons this out. He sees more of the reasons why they chose him. They must have known about his marital difficulties, he thinks. They must have figured he would be smart enough to realize that he wasn't meant to come home, and that it would be easier for a depressed man to accept a hopeless fate. But David is not overly bitter about being used this way. He understands that the one chance to save the human race rests with him. On the other hand, he isn't happy about being on a suicide mission. He doesn't want to die—not yet. He searches the ship and finds a bomb built into one of the walls. It is the real bomb—the one with the antimatter in it. The bomb they handed him was a fake.

"David is smarter than his superiors suspected. He disarms the bomb and removes it from the wall. He adjusts it so that he, and only he, can detonate it when he wishes. About this time they are closing on the alien home world. In fact, it has become visible up ahead."

My father stopped. I waited for him to continue; I was enjoying the story, although, as I said, I had heard parts of it before. But I soon realized my father had stopped for a good reason.

"That's as far as you've gotten," I said.

He nods. "Yeah. Pathetic, isn't it?"

"Not at all. You have me captivated."

"Thank you. I know you are not just telling me that.

I like the beginning of the story as well. The problem is, if you captivate the audience, you've got to give them their money's worth before you let them go. I have all the pieces of a great science-fiction epic, yet I don't know what my story's about."

"It's about the war, the struggle for survival, between the aliens and the humans."

He shook his head. "You're smarter than that. For it to work it has to have an underlying theme. I have no theme. I have no clear path of action. I don't know what David will do when he gets to the home world. I don't know what Vani will do. I don't understand the aliens at all. I don't know why they destroyed the Earth, except that it was the single act that started the war, and that is the one act I know I can't change. Really, I don't even know why David's wife left him. I feel her, Josie, I do. She was devoted to him."

I asked delicately. "Is she Mom?"

He shrugged. "She lives on a planet far away, far in the future. I suppose if you believe in reincarnation she could be your mother."

"That's not what I meant."

"I know," he said softly. We sat and stared at the waves. The orange light on the horizon turned gray. Out at sea, Delos faded to black. The wind continued to gain strength. "Do you have any ideas?" my dad finally asked.

I took a moment to answer. I *knew* this story. My father and I were alike in that way. We didn't believe stories were thought up. We felt they were uncovered. I felt my dad had begun to dust away a tale that had already been told—in another time and place. As he spoke of the characters, I had a sense of their reality. The story would come out, I knew it would, but in its own time.

"I do have a few ideas," I said. "But I'd like to think about them for a while. Would that be all right?"

"Take as long as you like. I am."

I laughed and stood up. "We're not living on the streets yet. What are you doing this evening?"

"Silk and I are going to dinner later. Oh, I meant to tell you, before I got carried away talking about the movie, Helen said she'd meet you at the Table, which is a restaurant in town. She said you walk in on the main street, then turn right when you come to the fork in the road. She said she'd meet you at ten." He checked his watch. "Which is in ten minutes."

"Helen will wait for me." The directions were not precise, but I figured if I got lost I could always ask around. "Do you want Helen and me to join you?"

My dad gave me a knowing look. "You two don't want to be saddled with us when you're flirting with boys." His face grew serious. "I heard you swam out too far this afternoon and almost drowned."

That Helen, I thought, what a mouth. I brushed the remark aside with my hand. "I got a little cramp is all. It was nothing."

"Did you have any pain in your chest?"

"No. The cramp was in my right hamstring." I leaned over and kissed his cheek. "Don't worry about me. Nothing can kill me. I'm immortal."

He was reassured. "Parents would like to think that's true of their children. But still, Josie, be careful next time."

I started for the door. "I will. I'll see you tomorrow morning."

"Good. We'll go exploring together."

I avoided the lounge on the way out so that I didn't have to talk to Silk again. My scooter keys were in my pocket, but I was reluctant to take the bike into town. I knew I would have to park it at the edge of the city. Most of the streets of Hora were as narrow as sidewalks, and Helen had already warned me that people didn't appreciate having to jump out of the way of bikes. The town was close. Taking the bike would only gain me ten minutes. Also, I was thinking of doing a little drinking, and could see myself driving off the road and into the water, and how much Helen would have to talk about then. I figured it would be best if I walked.

The road into town had no lights, but the moon, nearly full, had risen, and it provided me with all the illumination I needed. I could see better than most people at night. The wind in my hair was a treat. The town up ahead was lit as if for a holiday. But as Mr. Politopulos said, every day on Mykonos was a holiday. Even before I arrived, I could feel the energy of the night life. People were drinking, chasing each other, but there was also romance in the air. I wouldn't mind coming to Mykonos on my honeymoon, I thought—if I ever got married, that was.

I entered Hora and made my way over the cobblestones of the main road. Every building was whitewashed, and everywhere there were people, gorgeous people clad in shorts, jeans, halter tops, and T-shirts. I saw a few Americans, but fewer than I would have imagined. There were plenty of Greeks, of course, and tons of French, Italian, and English people. Most of them were with dates, and I wondered if Tom and Pascal were already with Helen.

But the boys were not at the restaurant when I caught up with my friend. The seating was outside, beneath a canopy. Helen sat alone at a corner table, lit with a candle in a jug, a bottle of wine in her hand. She greeted me with a smile and quickly answered my unspoken questions.

"Tom and Pascal should be here in half an hour," Helen said. "Tom wanted to wait for Pascal, and he doesn't get off work till now."

"What does he do?"

"I don't know. But these jobs are just summer work for these guys so they can live here and chase tourists like us." She nodded to her bottle, which looked to be approximately a pint. She had finished half of it. "This is *retsina,* the favorite wine here. If you order a bottle, watch your brain cells. It's strong medicine."

I signaled to the waiter. "I can handle it."

"I don't want you to wake up with a headache."

"No problem," I said. The waiter arrived and I pointed to the bottle and held up a finger. I didn't know if he spoke English, but he understood my sign language.

44

"How are you feeling?" Helen asked.

"I slept too long. I'll be up all night. I wish you'd awakened me."

"You looked tired."

"Most people do when they're asleep," I said.

"How are you feeling? How's your chest?"

"I'm perfectly fine. Let's not talk about this afternoon around the guys."

Helen nodded. "I won't bring it up if Tom doesn't."

"Tom won't bring it up."

Helen raised an eyebrow. "So you know him that well already."

I shrugged. "Whatever."

Helen set down her bottle and leaned closer. "I like him, Josie. I just wanted to tell you that."

I was annoyed. "I'm not going to steal him away from you, if that's what you mean."

"I doubt you could steal him away."

"Then what are you worried about?"

"Who said I'm worried?" Helen asked.

"No one, Helen. We are arguing about nothing. Let's stop."

"No. If you like Tom, and he prefers you, I don't mind. I'm just saying I like him. Nothing more. But he's fair game."

She was lying through her teeth, but I was tired of discussing it. I leaned back in my chair, yawning. "If that's the way you want it, fine. But I'm sure I'll love Pascal."

The boys showed up fifteen minutes later. By then I was halfway through my own bottle of wine and feeling fine. Tom had changed into black jeans that could have just come off the rack and a green sweat shirt with short sleeves. His brown sun-bleached hair was combed and he had on black leather shoes. He looked, as they say in England, smashing, and I was happy he was fair game.

Pascal was a hunk. He had to be six four, two hundred pounds, and most of it muscle. He was dark, his eyebrows thick as midnight woods, his eyes deep as European history. He looked sensual and dangerous, a smoldering presence. He sat beside me after first asking with his expression if it was OK. Tom sat beside Helen. He introduced Pascal, who nodded. Helen did the honors for us.

"I hope you two haven't been waiting long," Tom said. "Pascal doesn't get off work till ten."

"What do you do, Pascal?" I asked, not sure how the words were being received. But Pascal straightened himself and nodded again.

"I work with *legumes*—vegetables—for the city. I carry on my back, the *legumes.*"

His accent was not like someone's from Paris. I knew a few of those from my father's connections in Hollywood, and I suspected Pascal was from the countryside, maybe southern France.

"In America I work with a cook, a caterer," I said.

He listened, then nodded. "You cook *legumes?*" he asked.

I smiled. "All kinds of things."

Tom rubbed his hands together. "I would like to eat

all kinds of things. I'm starving. Let see, at this place the chicken is great. But if you're adventurous, have some of the local specialties. There're *melopittes*— small tarts made of dough, honey, and *tyrovolia; louza*—sausages made of pork and aromatic greens; and *amygdalota*—sweets made of crushed almonds."

"What are you having?" Helen asked.

"Fish and chips," Tom said matter-of-factly.

"Steak," Pascal said. I suppose he was tired of *legumes.*

"I want one of everything you just mentioned," I said.

"You don't even know what that stuff looks like," Helen said.

"I'll eat with my eyes closed if I don't like the look of it," I replied. Tom and Pascal laughed. Helen studied the menu. She was a picky eater.

"I feel like some chicken," she finally said.

The waiter took our orders and the guys got their own bottles of wine. We made a number of toasts: to ourselves, to world peace, to the island of Mykonos. Then I toasted the ancient gods. Tom stared at me when I made that toast.

"If you are interested in learning about ancient Greece you should visit Delos," Tom said. "Boats leave for it every morning at eight and at nine. I've been there a couple of times. It's fascinating—all the ruins."

"We were planning to go tomorrow morning," Helen said.

"Can you come with us?" I asked.

Pascal shook his head. "I have to work," Tom said, and he turned to Helen. "I remember last time you were here. You visited Delos regularly."

Helen paused. "A couple of times. I'm anxious to show it to Josie."

"Did you see any gods there?" I asked Helen, joking.

She stared at me. "No."

We drank more wine and talked and finally our food arrived. Mine looked delicious, and I ate with great relish, trying to force bits down Helen's throat, much to her annoyance. The waiter brought me a drink, *soumada,* made from crushed almonds. It was particularly good. Tom and I began to dominate the conversation. Pascal seemed content to listen and smile and get drunk. Helen was happy with her chicken—and, I hoped, with me. She had a habit of falling silent for lengthy periods. From experience, I had learned that such silences didn't necessarily mean she was depressed. On the other hand, they could. Helen's depression was not something I took lightly.

Therefore we had a problem on the way. As the evening proceeded it became obvious to me, and I think to Tom, that Josie and Tom were hitting it off nicely. Pascal was nice, handsome, adorable—but he was not my type. A guy had to have wit to capture my imagination. Ralphy Boy had been hilarious—when he wasn't busy feeding his fish, which is what he had called our lovemaking. But Ralph's laughter had been stifled around Helen. He said it was the main reason he'd left her. He couldn't be himself. That was puzzling, of course, because Helen could be funny when she wanted to be. But she had to be in the mood.

Helen was not making many jokes that night. We finished our food and hit the streets. Tom suggested we walk to the harbor. We moved as a group—it was hard to say who was with whom. I was happy for the guides. Hora was a labyrinth of crisscrossing paths, a maze of narrow alleys. Tom said that the first time he entered Hora he had to spend the night because he couldn't find his way out.

"About four in the morning, you see all the drunk tourists staggering around trying to find their way back to their hotels," Tom said. "I swear, a special service to retrieve them would make a fortune."

"Why don't you start such a service?" I asked.

"Because I'm often drunk at that time myself," Tom said.

"It is me who am *ivre*," Pascal said. "Tom has to find home for me."

"How many months out of the year do you work here?" I asked.

"Just during tourist season," Tom said. "From June to September. The rest of the time I'm in school."

"Where do you go?" I asked.

"Oxford," Tom said.

"He is genius," Pascal said. "All his teachers love Tom."

"What do you do the rest of the year?" Helen asked

Pascal. He had been giving Helen the most attention, perhaps sensing that I was interested in Tom, and vice versa.

"With *paralyze*—crippled children," he said. "In a school in the country. Many can't walk. Some have trouble—talking."

"Do you have a degree in that?" Helen asked.

Pascal shook his head and acted slightly confused. "I take care of them." He smiled. "They like me. I like them."

Tom spoke. "Pascal is a wonder with children. They think he walks on water. When my nieces and nephews met him they forgot their uncle was even there."

"How do you two know each other?" I asked.

"From here," Tom said.

Pascal laughed. "From the *vin.*"

"What?" I asked.

"From the wine," Tom said.

"What are you majoring in?" I asked Tom.

He shrugged. He seemed reluctant to talk about his academic achievements, perhaps, I thought, because he was humble. I knew Oxford wasn't easy to get into.

"I don't know," he said. "Our system is different from yours. I enjoy literature, which is a wide field, of course. I sometimes dream of staying here and becoming a fisherman."

"I can understand that," I said, enjoying the music pouring out from every food joint and bar. "I don't know if I'll ever leave."

We reached the water a few minutes later. Inside the walls of the buildings, we had been protected from the breeze, but once out in the open the wind swept through my hair. The harbor, however, was well protected from the ocean, and the many anchored boats rocked easily. Along the waterway were another dozen bars and restaurants. The whole town was geared for tourism, which Tom said was the lifeblood of the island. The place was dead in the winter, he told us.

Tom and Pascal led us north, away from the hustle and bustle of Hora. Helen wondered at this.

"Where are we going?" she asked.

"I thought we might walk to where the ferries come in," Tom said. "Pascal bought a used truck on the mainland and it's supposed to arrive sometime this week. It could come in on a boat tonight."

Pascal nodded. *"Camion* for work. Save *le dos*— 'back' for better things."

The moon had risen high by now, and the brilliant silver light had transformed the ocean water into a mystical brew worthy of a titan's thirst. Our path, at first, took us up, so that the harbor was laid out below us, then back down again toward the water. When Tom had first used the word *ferry* I'd had the image in my mind of a small boat. But when Tom pointed out to sea at the gigantic vessel approaching the island, decked in what could have been a mile-long string of yellow Christmas lights, I realized I was being foolish. I had read in Helen's book about the ferries that went from island to island, how they transported literally hundreds of cars along with their passengers. This incoming boat was as huge as an ocean liner.

It moved with amazing speed and precision. We were barely back down to the water when it plowed into the north side of the harbor, sending out powerful waves that rocked the pleasure boats docked on the other side of the bay. For a moment the ferry seemed to stand still, before suddenly pivoting on its axis and neatly sliding into the wide slot allotted for it. The entire docking procedure took only minutes. The end of the vessel split open, a garage door several stories tall descending onto the shore. Soon a horde of cars was pouring from the bowels of the vessel. Half the drivers looked as if they had already been drinking on neighboring islands.

"Boats like this run night and day between all the main Greek islands," Tom said.

"Have you been to many of the others?" I asked.

"Yeah," Tom said. "Corfu, Santorini—there are a lot of them. But I'm always happy to get back to Mykonos."

"Why's that?" I asked.

"There's just something here," he said. "A good feeling."

I nodded. "I know what you mean."

"It comes from Delos," Helen said suddenly. We glanced at her. "You'll see tomorrow, Josie."

"I'm intrigued," I said.

Pascal's truck was on the boat. Apparently a Greek associate of his had helped bring it over from Athens. Pascal hailed him as he rolled off the massive ramp. The guy did not stay with us, though, not after he got his money from Pascal, an envelope with God only knew how many drachmas in it. He disappeared into the night.

The truck was a sad affair. It looked as if it had been driven underwater and taken a few years to arrive. The paint was peeling, the front bumper was ready to kiss the ground, and the tires could have been balloons painted with tread to pass for Michelins. But Pascal was delighted to see it, shaking his keys with excitement. He pointed to his back before he climbed inside the two-seater front compartment.

"Bags of *legumes*—heavy," he said. "Need *le camion*—truck."

So we lost Pascal then. He wanted to drive his *camion,* and no one wanted to go with him. As he sped away, Helen gave me a glance like it might not be a bad time for me to get lost as well. But the subtlety of it was deliberately lost on me, Tom being fair game and all. I was having too much fun, but maybe I wouldn't have been such a bitch about it if the wine hadn't loosened my stride and my mouth. I knew I would pay for it the next day with a hangover and Helen's bad humor, but sometimes a little pain was a good investment. In fact, I felt like another bottle of wine. Tom looked at both of us, as if he was about to get in double trouble.

"What would you ladies like to do now?" he asked.

I think both of us would have liked to have sex with him, but we were too proper to say so. Helen continued to stare at me as if I might dematerialize under the power of her gaze. But I was a happy-go-lucky California babe.

"Let's go get drunk," I said.

"You never get drunk," Helen protested. "You hate drunks. You hate Silk."

"I am a young lithe female jam-filled with contradictions," I said.

Tom laughed. "We're all going to hate ourselves in the morning, but I know a great bar buried in the center of the city. It's off the main alleyways, located a few stories up. You have to know exactly where it is and follow a winding route to find it. But the atmosphere is brilliant."

"I think you use the word *brilliant* different from us," I said. "It's not *smart*, is it? It's more like *bitchin'*, isn't it? I want to go there."

"You should rest after that attack you had today," Helen said.

I gave her a look. "I was not 'attacked.' I was 'rescued.' They are completely opposite things."

We went to the bar. Tom had been right. It was buried deep in the city, off the beaten paths. The atmosphere was more subdued, the music low. We took a booth by the window, the north wind a caress on our sleeves. Helen was definitely not happy with me. While Tom and I ordered more wine, she asked for a Scotch and soda. She was going to try to drink me under the table. Did she think Tom would be impressed? I didn't know. I honestly didn't understand Helen at all, and I had grown up with her. Lately I had begun to think we weren't even friends. The fault wasn't with her alone, I realized, but with both of us. We didn't look out for each other. I was always stealing her boys and she was always competing with me on issues of sheer stupidity. Oh well, I thought, if she won in the hangover department, she was welcome to it.

I knew I hadn't been looking out for Helen the previous summer, that was for sure. It was good her parents had taken her to Greece, to get away from it all—whatever had caused her to do what she had to herself. To this day I still don't know all the details. Maybe I hadn't wanted to know. I got sick right after that. Helen had only returned from Greece the day I was released from the hospital.

When we met that day, it was as if we were seeing each other for the first time. We both looked like hell.

Our conversation started well enough in the bar with no name. It was more balanced, for a while. Helen even told a couple of obscene jokes, and Tom described what Oxford was like for a poor undergraduate on a scholarship. But Helen quickly had three Scotch and sodas in a row, then she was just blubbering. She started to talk about how awesome Tom's body was, how *brilliant* his ass was in his shorts, especially when they were wet. Tom tried to act as if nothing was amiss, he was so polite, but when Helen suddenly whipped her head to the side, and opened her mouth, and let out a loud gagging sound, followed by a half gallon of—yuck.

Helen *vomited* on the floor.

It was a tragedy of Greek proportions.

She even splashed Tom's sandals.

No way to impress a guy, I thought.

"Damn," Helen kept whispering as she wiped at her face. "Damn, damn, damn." She looked at us miserably, and she was tranquilized. She would feel much worse in the morning. "I'm sorry, Tom."

I can't believe what he said next. "It happens to the best of us."

Our waitress arrived and saw the mess on the floor. She looked like she was going to be sick next. I raised my bottle to my lips and finished my wine. Definitely an interesting evening, I thought. I must have been drunk as well. I couldn't even smell the puke. Thank God the waitress didn't speak English. She turned and fled. Helen watched her leave, perplexed.

"I think I should go home," she mumbled.

Tom stood up. He wouldn't be returning to this bar soon. He took Helen by the arm and helped her to her feet. "We'll all go home now," he said.

Tom helped her outside, but I took Helen after that. Tom gave me a quick pat on the back as he said goodbye. I wished it had been on my butt, his hand, I was feeling like such a loose woman. I burst into giggles and tried to kiss him. Helen fell on the ground and started crying. Tom fairly ran away. Wonderful fun.

I howled at the moon. "I love Greece!" I shouted.

Helen crawled at my feet. "I hate it," she grumbled.

I don't know how we made it back to the hotel. There must have been a special Greek god who watched over drunks. It was the only logical explanation.

Sometime during the night I dreamed. I walked in a garden of light. There were grass meadows, populated by flowers of fragrance, branches of shade hanging like gentle arms from trees of antiquity, streams of water flowing with honey—paradise, and everything was suffused with a soft blue light. The glow penetrated my skin, warming my blood, making it tingle as it flowed through my veins. For I too shone with the light, a radiant being. My white robe was long, cast over only one shoulder, the left, the right one bare, free to hold a bow and arrow.

This paradise was tranquil. My steps took me beside a pool of liquid, and I knelt and caught my reflection and for a moment lost my breath. Because, truly, I was beautiful beyond human measure, and even though the face did not belong to Josie, I recognized the nose, the mouth, the eyes, especially the eyes—blue jewels of the heavens, stolen from the rays of the sun as they burst off the lip of a crashing wave.

The face of the goddess was familiar to me.

I awoke with a start in the depth of night, surrounded by black. Helen slept peacefully beside me on the adjoining bed. My stomach was settled. There was no pain in my head. It was as if the alcohol had entered my bloodstream and exited by a way that bypassed my liver. I remembered my dream with startling clarity.

"Maybe the blue light saved me from the drink," I whispered.

It was a pleasant thought.

I lay down and went back to sleep.

CHAPTER 3

THE NEXT MORNING FOUND HELEN, SILK, MY DAD, AND ME on a rather large boat heading for Delos. We were on the nine o'clock, not the eight, and we were lucky to have made it. We were all wearing sunglasses, but I was the only one not hiding bloodshot eyes. I had awakened completely free of a hangover. Such could not be said for the others. Silk and my dad sat huddled close together, as if they could protect each other from the rocking of the boat. Helen was a little apart from them, closer to me, with her head bent over so far it was practically between her knees. She groaned as we cleared the harbor area and entered the open sea. Here there were waves, churning four footers, rocking the boat from side to side.

"How long does it take to get there?" I asked Helen.

"Twenty-five minutes," she replied.

"That isn't bad."

"Speak for yourself."

"You'd feel even worse if you hadn't vomited most of it up before you went to bed," I said, trying to sound cheerful.

Helen raised her head wearily. "Gimme a break."

"Tom was pretty drunk himself. He won't even remember that you heaved all over the floor."

Helen put a hand to her head. "Please don't use the word *heave* right now."

"I'm sorry."

"He won't have to remember," Helen said with a sigh. "He'll just have to put his sandals on and it'll all be there for him." She eyed me suspiciously. "I guess we know who made the better impression."

"It's not a contest."

Helen put her head back down. "All of life is a contest."

Delos was located about one nautical mile from Mykonos, but because the port of Hora was located more on the north side of Mykonos, while Delos lay to the west, the boat had to travel approximately four miles to reach the sacred island. I had purchased a small pamphlet about Delos and sat down beside Helen to read about where I would be spending my morning.

Delos

Uninhabited today, Delos was one of the most revered religious centers of the Greek world. Legend connects it with the birth of Apollo, god of light and prophesy.

Homer in his "Hymn to Apollo" recounts how Leto, in desperation, searched everywhere for a place to give birth to the child of her secret affair with Zeus, king of the gods. Everywhere she went, she was turned away, because no spirit dared risk the wrath of Hera, the wife of Zeus. But when Leto finally reached Delos, she said to the island, "So poor is your earth, what man could be induced to set foot here? Neither cow nor sheep can graze here, neither grapevines nor any form of tree will ever prosper on you, such is the dryness that scourges you. But if my son were born here, then you could nurture your people, because the beasts that men would bring here to be sacrificed would be beyond counting." Leto swore on the holy water of the Styx that the god about to be born would never forget the barren island and that he would found his foremost sanctuary there.

In addition to this myth, the lyric poet Pindar mentioned that Delos was an island that floated in the Aegean, traveling here and there with no fixed location. The mortals called it Ortygia, the gods Asteria, because from afar it shone like a star. As soon as Leto set foot on Delos, four columns rose out of the deep, fixing the island in place so that it never moved again. . . .

I enjoyed the myth very much. A goddess searching for a place to have her child, the son of the king of the gods, and an island that floated through the night and shone like a star. The name Delos came from the Greek word *A-delos,* which means the invisible one. How perfectly wonderful, I thought, if such things were really true.

Of course, I knew they were only stories. Still . . .

The pamphlet went on to describe the island's history in detail. The Ionians first made Delos their religious headquarters in about 1000 B.C. Regular festivals were held in honor of Apollo and his sister Artemis. After a few hundred years the Athenians came and took over Delos, but the worship of Apollo continued. Near the turn of the millennium, the Romans ransacked the island, pillaging and murdering, and destroying. Raids by pirates completed the destruction, and Delos was all but forgotten, once more "invisible." In 1872 the French School of Archaeology at Athens began its systematic excavations of the island, which were still underway.

I set aside the pamphlet. Helen wanted to know if I had an aspirin. I searched in my purse, finding a bottle of Tylenol. I handed her two.

"Should I get you a glass of water?" I asked.

Helen popped the pills into her mouth and swallowed. "It doesn't matter."

"We could have gone to Delos tomorrow," I said. "We have all week." It was Helen, even with a hangover, who had awakened us all that morning and insisted we make the nine o'clock boat.

"Our vacation will be gone before you know it," Helen said. "We're only allowed on the island till one. Then they kick everyone off. I can rest all afternoon."

"Will we be able to see most of the island in that time?"

"Yes. It's not very big."

Immediately across from tiny Delos was another island, Rheneia, which was about four times the size of Delos. Our boat plowed through the channel between the two islands and docked at a small harbor on the west side of Delos, close to the ruins of the ancient city. There was only one other boat in the area: the eight o'clock tourist cruiser, for less-than-heavy drinkers.

I was excited. The pictures of Delos in my pamphlet had not fully conveyed the scope of the ruins. Here was a genuine city from the past. I hurried down the gangplank, practically pulling Helen. I wouldn't explore the island in the company of my father and Silk. Dad was out of shape and Silk had as much feel for history as a dog.

As a group we were funneled through a gate. Incredibly, on top of the boat fare, we had to spring for another five hundred drachmas to get in. It wasn't a lot of money, but it annoyed me. I mean, what if I hadn't brought extra? What would I do then, sit on the boat for a few hours? They gave us one-page maps and advised us to team up with a guide, but Helen steered me away from them.

"They spit on you if you take too many pictures," she whispered. "Especially if you're a filthy American."

I laughed. "At least they don't vomit on you like some of us."

"Your time will come," Helen promised me.

We got on an ancient stone path, made of dusty white marble slabs, and veered to the left, walking north. First, according to our little map, we passed the Stoa of Philip, built in 210 B.C. by Philip V of Macedon as an offering to Apollo, and on the right was the South Stoa, a third century B.C. building probably paid for by a king of Pergamon.

"What's a stoa?" I asked Helen.

"Beats me."

Next came the Temple of Apollo, his sanctuary. It was actually three temples grouped together. The oldest, Porinos Naos, was constructed of sandstone; the middle one was made of marble; and the last, the most impressive, was the Temple of the Delians. It was the only temple on the island with a colonnade on all sides, and it dominated the sanctuary. As I stepped inside it and placed my hand on one of the standing marble pillars, I felt an odd sensation shoot up my arm, almost as if an electrical current had been released through my nerves. I quickly withdrew my hand and stared at it.

"You're not supposed to touch the pillars," Helen said, but her voice was not disapproving. Rather, she was watching to see if I would do it again. I obliged her—the stone felt cool, even in the direct sun. Yet I noticed no current this time.

"That was odd," I whispered.

"What happened?" Helen asked.

"For a moment I felt as if . . ." I shrugged, removing my hand. I did not have words for the experience, because what I had felt was that the stone had greeted me, which was, of course, absurd.

We continued on. Next came the Terrace of the Lions. I had seen pictures of these guys in the pamphlet, and I was happy to meet them—a row of stone lions, each on his own stone block. Helen and I cornered another tourist and had him take our picture —using my new expensive camera—standing beside one of the beasts.

We explored farther north, walking in and out of ruins with names I was never going to remember. Slowly, steadily, I began to soak up the atmosphere of the island and began to understand what had captivated Helen about the place. There was something magical, a sense of enchantment. I felt somehow *cleansed* by the island, as if there were gods standing above us in the sky, smiling down.

Walking in the bright sun, we were struck with a sudden thirst. Helen led me back the way we had come, then east, in the direction of a long modern building, which was nestled at the foot of low hills, behind the ruins.

"It's a museum," Helen explained. "I don't care much for it myself, but there are some beautiful mosaics inside if you want to have a peek. There's a snack bar next to it. We can get sodas there."

"I could drink a six-pack right now," I said.

We went to the snack bar first. I downed two Cokes quickly and accidentally let out a horrendous belch. Others, sophisticated European types, scowled—filthy Americans. I laughed and ordered another drink and a sandwich. Helen's hangover must have been easing up because she ate half my food without even asking permission.

Helen really didn't want to go inside the museum, which she had expanded upon until it became the bore of the millennium. I was easy. Helen pointed to the south end of the island where the ground rose steadily, until it suddenly shot up into a towering pinnacle.

"We want to go there," she said.

I consulted our map. "What's it called?"

Helen pulled away the map before I could get the name. "It's where Apollo was born," she said. She had removed her sunglasses. Her brown eyes were suddenly excited, although rimmed with red. The sun was hard on her. She was already low on sunscreen.

"Cool," I said. "Where he was conceived?"

Helen nodded, serious. "Some say so. It's a power spot. You'll feel it, like you did when you touched the pillar."

I froze for a moment. "How do you know I felt anything when I touched the pillar?" I asked softly.

"I saw it on your face," Helen said.

I didn't know what to make of that.

We finished our drinks and sandwich and set out for the pinnacle. Along the way we passed a number of other fascinating ruins, but now that we had a goal, they didn't hold my attention.

The incline sharpened. Then we were on a row of steps that wound up to the top. It was a natural hill, I could see that with my eyes, yet it somehow gave the impression of having been thrust up from the grounds, forced out, suddenly, by titanic forces. From a distance its height was deceptive, but plowing up the steps, panting, a hint of a cramp in the center of my chest, I realized how high it was. It seemed to take forever to reach the top.

Finally, though, we were at the summit, which we had to ourselves for the moment. The tourists hardy enough to make the climb had come here first and were already departing. The wind was strong, whistling in our ears, but the silence seemed to ring as well. Helen had been right. There was something undeniably powerful about the spot, a presence so palpable I would have felt I was being observed if it hadn't been so comforting.

The day was spectacularly clear. We could see for over a hundred miles in every direction. A number of the Cyclades, the circle of islands of which Delos and Mykonos were a part, were visible on the blue horizon. There was a mount upon the top of the hill itself, an inner circle of short, toppled marble pillars that would make better seats than supports. Helen led me to the center and told me to sit. I was still trying to catch my breath and was happy for the rest.

"You like it here," Helen said, not asking.

I nodded, shielding my eyes to gaze at the sky. The sun had never seemed so bright, even with my sunglasses on. It was as if it were pouring through a hole in the heavens that had been cut directly above us so that the sun's full glory could be appreciated. How wonderful the heat felt on my skin right then. For a moment I was reminded of my dream, the blue radiance soaking into my blood, setting it to song. Like that, the golden rays blazing down from the sky were a soothing balm for all my complaints, emotional as well as physical. And perhaps spiritual as well. Yes, I felt as if I were sitting in a place of holiness, where an act of divine origin had occurred in the distant past, but with effects still reverberating to the present. I felt this in my heart, even though I wasn't a religious person.

I never wanted to leave the spot.

"I like it," I told Helen, and I closed my eyes and lay back against a stone. Helen came and sat beside me. I sensed her without looking.

"When I got out of the hospital last summer," she said, "I knew I had to come here to get well. I pestered my parents until they agreed. Then I did just what you're doing. I lay down and soaked up the sun and let the gods talk to me."

"Did you have your sunblock on during this conversation?" I mumbled, feeling suddenly sleepy. The sun could do that.

"Yes." Helen was silent for a time. "Afterward I didn't feel like a nut case who had tried to take her life. I felt strong. I felt alive."

I opened my eyes. We had never directly spoken of her suicide attempt. I didn't even know how she had tried to end her life, except that her parents had thought I was partly to blame for the attempt. Silly them—I did wonder if it had something to do with the whole Ralph thing.

"I hope this place does as much for you now," I said sincerely.

Helen touched my hand. She seldom touched me. "I am more curious about what it does for you. You were sick as well last summer."

"But I'm all better now," I said quickly. I didn't know what Helen was getting at.

"Time is strange when you're sick, Josie. Particularly when you're burning with fever. A minute can seem like days. The reverse is also true. Years can go by in a flash."

Now I was watching her. "You just described what happened to me when I was in the hospital. How did you know I felt that way?"

She shrugged. "It's common when you have a fever."

"I suppose." I sat up and let her hand fall away from mine. "How did you know you should come here? How did you know it would be good for you? You were never interested in Greek culture until then."

Helen stared down at the ancient city, at the other tourists moving in and around the bleached ruins like so many ants scurrying around scattered piles of sugar. The people were so small, viewed from this Olympian height, small and powerless. But it was the place, I reminded myself, that held the special magic, not us. I wondered if Helen realized that.

"I just knew," Helen said.

"That's no answer."

She wouldn't meet my eyes. "Things change when you almost die. You know that."

She had caught me off guard because of what she said. It was true, of course. My life had undergone a dramatic shift since I almost passed on. Yet she hadn't answered my question, at least I didn't think she had.

In the distance we heard our boat blow its horn. It was time to head back. I got to my feet, wiping at my shorts. What happened next—I don't know what brought it on. It may have been that I got up too quickly, and the blood fell from my brain to my toes. In any case, I saw a sudden flash of light and then for an instant, almost no light. It was as if for a moment I was standing above Delos, viewing the buildings in the silver glow of the full moon, rather than under the scorching glare of the midday sun. That wasn't all, though. The buildings had also changed.

They were new again. All of them.

I blinked. The sun returned.

It had been a hallucination.

The ruins—they were as they had been for centuries.

I staggered against Helen. She caught me before I could fall.

"What's wrong?" she asked.

I wiped at my eyes. "Nothing."

"Are you sure? Are you strong enough to walk back down?"

I remembered her remark of a moment before. *I felt strong. I felt alive.*

"I feel strong," I said.

We started down the hill.

CHAPTER 4

EVERYONE WAS EAGER TO REST WHEN WE RETURNED TO OUR hotel after our visit to Delos, except me. I was confused about my strange experiences on the sacred island, but one thing I knew for sure. I was pumped with energy to spare. Snorkeling gear flung over my back, I got on my motorbike, gave it a macho kick, heard the engine roar to life, and was on my way to explore new parts of Mykonos.

Of course, I first headed straight to Paradise Beach to see if Tom was working. I was fortunate on two accounts. He was at the bar and he was on his break. He didn't seem surprised to see me, although his greeting was warm. I noticed he had on new sandals.

"How's your head today?" I asked, sitting on the stool beside him. I had on my naughtiest bathing suit under my shorts and blouse, a blue bikini that could have been stuffed into a contact lens case. Tom nodded toward the glass of milk he was drinking.

"It gets better as the day goes on. As long as I don't think about it. How are you?"

"Splendid. Wild time last night," I offered.

He smiled, always the gentleman. "I had fun."

"Want to do it again tonight?"

He hesitated. "Does Helen?"

"Does Pascal?"

He laughed. "Are you trying to put the two of them together?"

I was bold. "It's better than tearing you and Helen apart."

He shrugged. "She's just a friend. Nothing happened between us last summer."

"Does she know that?" I shook myself. "I'm sorry, I shouldn't put you on the spot. But you see, the situation's awkward for me. I want to see you tonight, if I can, but I don't want to upset my friend, or you."

He came to my aid, poor bleeding soul that I was. "I would like to see you tonight as well, Josie. I understand the problems here. But if it is of any help, I think Pascal likes Helen. He wanted her to go with him in his truck last night."

"I don't think Helen cares much for that *le camion*."

"How about Pascal?" he asked.

"I'm afraid she's got her heart set on an English mate." I paused, thinking—or, rather, plotting. All right, so I was acting horribly bitchy. What was I

73

supposed to do? I liked Tom and he liked me. Why should I deprive myself just because it might hurt Helen? I asked myself.

There were good answers to both those questions.

Do nothing—because Helen was my friend and deserved my loyalty.

It was hard to make such commitments with Tom sitting only a foot away. He looked so delicious. I felt like Judas.

"Why don't the two of you run into us at the same restaurant at the same time as last night," I suggested. "We can act like we never met this afternoon. Then we'll just take it from there."

"Why don't you just tell Helen you want to see me and leave it at that? You'll hurt her more with deception."

"Why don't you tell her?" I asked hopefully.

He shook his head. "If we 'just take it from there,' where will we go? We'll have a repeat of last night."

"Helen won't vomit on you again, I promise."

He grinned. "All right, but Helen isn't stupid. At some point in the night we'll have to go our separate ways, and she'll be upset."

"Tell Pascal to sweep her off her feet. Have him drag her away."

"I'll see what can be done." Tom checked his watch and stood up. "I have to get back to work. Don't swim out so far this time. I don't have the strength to rescue you today."

I touched his arm before he left. "I *was* in trouble

74

yesterday, and you may have saved my life. I didn't properly thank you for that."

He was humble. "I'm sure, had the situation been reversed, you would have done the same for me."

I held his eye a moment. I didn't know why, but his words chilled me to the bone. "That's true, Tom," I said softly.

I went snorkeling, but following his advice, I stayed close to shore. The water felt good on my skin after the baking on Delos. I was thinking about going back to the sacred island the next day. It had a hold on me already—some kind of magnetic pull.

After a good long swim, I lay on the beach and took off my top and waited for all the men to faint. But mine were just another couple of perky breasts, and Paradise was filled with them. I wondered, as I lay there, if Tom could see me. Back home my figure had been the envy of many. But here I was just part of the scenery.

I didn't see Tom when I left the beach. I didn't know where he was.

At the hotel I found my father sitting by the pool, his laptop nearby, but closed. He said that Silk and Helen were still resting. It was after six already. Unlike yesterday, the wind was dying as the twilight deepened. I had talked to my father about Delos on the boat on the way back, leaving out my peculiar experiences. He had enjoyed the island immensely and said he wanted to go back soon. Silk had thought the place was run down.

"I was snorkeling on the other side of the island," I said, setting down my gear on the deck at my father's feet. I plopped down beside it. The pool was filled with ocean water, salty—Mr. Politopulos said it was hard to keep a freshwater pool from growing algae on Mykonos.

"You took your motor scooter?" Dad asked.

"Yeah. It's a blast. You're going to have to buy me a Harley-Davidson when we get back to L.A."

"I used to have a motorcycle when I was young. I used to love going out late on warm summer evenings and cruising Pacific Coast Highway." He shook his head. "I loved that bike."

"Why did you give it up?"

"I hit an oil spot flying through Topanga Canyon. I was doing eighty. The bike went over the side of the cliff. I was lucky I didn't. Scared the hell out of me. I never bought another bike." He paused. "Your mother made me swear I wouldn't."

"You knew her then?"

"We had just met."

"The good old days," I said. It was not often he talked about Mom. She left when I was ten. Now when I thought of her, she was like someone else's mother. She didn't even come to visit me in the hospital when I was sick. But then, maybe she didn't know. My father never talked to her.

"Yeah," my dad said. "Who would have thought then we would have ended the way we did? Our lawyers screaming at each other in a trashy divorce court, us sitting so quietly, so properly on opposite ends of the room. We couldn't even bear to look at each other."

"Did you write today?" I asked.

"I rewrote some of the dialogue at the beginning of the script. But I wrote nothing new because I know nothing new."

"The wife of your hero was not going to leave him."

"What?" he asked.

"Jessica never intended to divorce David Herrick. There was no other man. The military people put her up to the lie. They wanted David to accept the dangerous mission."

A glimmer of light shone in my father's eyes. "That's true. You know her."

I nodded. "I know Jessica. So does the alien female—Vani. She's the one who will explain this to David just before they land on the alien home world."

"How can Vani understand Jessica so well from such a distance? Plus they're not even of the same race."

"I'm not sure, but David talks to Vani about Jessica frequently—you said so yourself. Maybe you can push the theme that a woman is a woman—no matter the genetic makeup."

My father was excited. "I love this, Josie. It fits. The intelligence agency of the System—they're the ones who tortured Vani's husband to death. They would stoop to such an act." He stopped and scratched his head. "Now what do David and Vani do when they land on the alien home world?"

"They can't just blow it up?" I asked.

"And perish with the world? No."

"I was joking, I know that." I stopped. "A big piece is still missing—the key to the whole thing."

"Still, this is a valuable insight." My father leaned over and gave me a hug. "You are the genius in the family. If I sell this script, you must get a Guild credit."

"We can talk about that if I come up with the ending." I collected my gear and got up. "What are your plans for tonight?"

"To eat less and drink nothing. I heard you girls met a couple of guys?"

"Helen told you?"

"Yes. A French guy likes you?"

"Well, we'll see." I turned. "I'd better talk to Helen."

I found her in our bedroom. She was awake, reading one of my courtroom thrillers. Her face was sunburned—bad enough to peel.

"I wish you'd waked me up," she said. "Now I'm going to be up all night."

"I only just got back." I set down my snorkeling equipment.

"Where did you go?"

"I visited a few beaches I hadn't seen before."

"Which ones?" Helen asked, with a note of suspicion.

"I don't remember their names." I chuckled. "It was all Greek to me."

"Did you see Tom?"

"No. How could I see Tom?"

"I was just wondering. So you didn't go to Paradise?"

"I told you, no."

"No, you just told me that you didn't see Tom. I didn't know if you went to Paradise or not." Helen paused. "How's your chest?"

"My chest is fine. My breasts are getting a tan."

"You took off your top?"

"I almost took off my bottom. I think I will tomorrow."

"Are you hungry?" Helen asked. "I'd like to get something to eat."

It was a long time before we were supposed to meet Tom and Pascal at the restaurant. "No."

"You don't want to go into town?"

"Later."

"What are you going to do now?"

I sat down on my bed. "Rest for a while. Read."

"For how long?" she asked.

"I don't know."

"I was thinking of calling Tom, getting together with him later." She let the remark hang, waiting for me to respond. When I didn't, she asked, "Would you like him to see if Pascal's available?"

"I don't know. I think he was more interested in you than me."

"Is that another way of saying you're more interested in Tom than Pascal?" she asked.

Right then I almost told her that Tom and I had

already made plans. I would have if I could have started fresh, without all my lies behind me. I stretched out on the bed.

I yawned. "You have the imagination."

"You're the one with the imagination. I don't think your father can write a word without you."

I closed my eyes. "He wrote wonderfully well for many years when I was a little girl."

"You were there to help him," Helen said, her tone distant and disturbing. I refused to open my eyes. The more we talked, the more she'd see through me. Tom was right—Helen was not stupid. Her words followed me into my nap. *You were there to help him.* They made no sense to me, yet they rang with truth.

Once more I dreamed of paradise—not the beach, but the realm of the gods. Wearing my same white robe, I rode paths of sunlight that led to pleasure gardens unimaginable on the Earth below me. They could be found between the worlds, and they took on form as I passed through them on my way to my destination. Mount Olympus was vast, made up of many dimensions. Yet all these realities were connected. For all flowed from the sun, and had as their benefactor Apollo. Legend now said that he was born directly of the light from the eternal flame, and not from the loins of Zeus. But who could say with any certainty? Apollo wouldn't, he seldom spoke at all; and Zeus was long gone—to where no one knew.

But I did not ascend the staircase of the sun to seek pleasure but, rather, to worship at the secret altar of

Apollo that I had built for myself out of the material of mortal dreams. It existed on the dark side of the moon, and I had to pass into the shadow of that great orb to enter it. Ah, that was my great secret—that I worshiped the god of light in darkness. No one knew, except perhaps Apollo himself. But of that I wasn't certain. I only knew that when I paid him obeisance, my power to create grew very great.

I found my altar empty. The flowers I had left on my previous visit were dust that stirred on the cold wind that blew for all time from the empty blackness of space. I had brought fresh flowers with me, from the gardens of Leto, and these I placed on my altar as I bent my head low and prayed humbly for fresh dreams to give to my human devotees, visions to replace the ones I had taken from them. Visions of love and laughter, of song and dance, of adventures bold and beautiful—enough to stir life in the depth of even the most oppressed soul. The gods needed them as much as the mortals, if not more. . . .

CHAPTER 5

MY VISION WAS STILL WITH ME HOURS LATER AS I SAT WITH Helen at the corner table in the restaurant. It was only a dream to me, and I was feeling far from godlike. The time for Tom and Pascal to arrive was near. Helen was having chicken again. Me, too. In my heart I realized it was not going to work. Helen was going to find out about Tom and me, be heartbroken, hate me, hate herself, then maybe jump off a cliff. Still, I felt the situation was out of my control. I could not deny myself even a taste of love. It was against my nature— the rationale of a godlike ego, I knew, but a fact nevertheless.

The young men appeared. Tom had on his sandals from the day before. He must have washed them. Pascal was in work clothes. I suspected he might have been dragged directly here from his job. Yet Helen

appeared happy to see them, and if she suspected
Tom's and my plan she didn't show it. Tom said, as we
rehearsed, that they just happened to be passing. They
sat beside us and ordered food, Tom on Helen's side,
Pascal on mine. Tom had chicken, but Pascal was a
red meat lover. A bottle of wine appeared and we
toasted our good health and happiness.

The conversation flowed differently from the previous night. Helen was not letting Tom go without a
fight. She made every effort to keep his attention,
smiling at each of his words, nodding enthusiastically
when it was appropriate—and even when it was
not—and laughing too loudly if he made the slightest
witty remark. Clearly, she was making Tom uncom-
fortable. I tried to balance the unnaturalness in the
talk but had limited success. I wanted Tom's attention
as well, and it was hard to draw Pascal out. I don't
think it was the language barrier alone, because his
English was not that bad. He was simply quiet. He did
tell us about a crippled boy he took care of at his
school.

"His name is Samuel," Pascal said in his thick
accent. "Nice, nice boy—*dix ans*—ten years old.
Paralyzed—waist down. Car accident, very sad. But
Samuel can use hands. He start to paint when he got
to the school after hospital. I purchased him paints,
showed him how to use. In the beginning he paint
messy kids' things. But he get better fast. He begin to
paint trees outside school, the autos, and flowers.
Then he paint, ah, what you call faces?"

"Portraits," Tom said, listening carefully. He was always quick to defer to Pascal when his French friend spoke, perhaps because it was so seldom. It was interesting to watch the subtleties of their relationship. It was clear to me that Pascal worshiped Tom and his clever mind, but how Tom saw Pascal, I wasn't sure. That he cared for him a great deal, even loved him, I had no doubt. Pascal nodded his appreciation for the word.

"Portraits," Pascal said, his English improving as he talked more. "Samuel did portraits. He did mine —very good, better than I look. He did nurses, doctors. He painted and painted—sitting in his wheelchair. He do nothing but paint pictures—all our faces, all day. He get better and better, every day. He get so good, we call art teacher to look at his paintings. The man comes. He is old. Samuel paints his portrait. The man sits, he watches. We showed Samuel's other pictures, but teacher not believe Samuel paint them. He says, boy is too little to be so good. But we laugh. Samuel paint the teacher and then the man is smiling. He says Samuel is a master. He has been taught by the masters. But Samuel's mother comes. She says to the teacher, my son never painted before the accident." Pascal shook his head. "It is mystery no one understands."

Pascal stopped abruptly. It was a fascinating story, and I wanted him to continue. Tom must have heard the story before. He lowered his head when Helen asked her question.

"What is Samuel doing now?" Helen asked.

Pascal looked pained. "His kidneys—they go bad. He died."

I grimaced. "That's horrible. You said he was only ten? It's a shame the world should lose such a great talent. He might have been another da Vinci."

Pascal spoke seriously. "Teacher say he was da Vinci."

"Something did change in Samuel when he was in his accident," Tom said quickly, almost as if in explanation. "I don't think medical science can explain it. It's almost as if, with the death of portions of his spinal cord, certain parts of his brain woke up."

"Was Samuel in a coma immediately after his accident?" I asked.

Tom explained the word *coma* to Pascal, who nodded. "At first he sleep so that they can't wake him," Pascal said.

"Why did you ask that?" Tom asked me.

I shrugged. "Just wondering."

"Tom had coma one—" Pascal began.

"Let's not talk about that," Tom interrupted.

Pascal nodded. "Sorry."

"What was it?" I asked.

Tom shrugged. "Nothing. Stupid bicycle accident." He cleared his throat and returned to the subject. "Samuel woke up a different person, that's for sure. At least according to his mother."

"You met the boy?" I asked.

"Yes," Tom said. "He painted my picture as well. I have it in my apartment in Oxford. Samuel was definitely inspired by something."

The conversation turned to other matters, though none so interesting as Samuel. Then our food and drink were done, and the trouble started, as if on cue. Seemed Pascal had to go back to work. Tom must have briefed him on the situation, but not thoroughly enough. Before standing up to leave, Pascal invited Helen to accompany him. He said in his stumbling English that she could drive around the island with him in his brand-new *camion* while he delivered *legumes* to the hotels. He honestly believed it would be a romantic evening for her, I think. Helen acted confused.

"Aren't you asking Josie?" she said to Pascal.

Pascal glanced at Tom as if for help. Tom remained impassive, probably the best thing he could do under the circumstances. Pascal flashed a warm smile and said, "I would like to go with you." There was feeling in his voice. He did honestly like her. But Helen could not hear the affection.

"I'm with Tom," she said flatly.

"I could show you—sights," Pascal said, giving it one more try.

Helen turned to me. "Why don't you go with Pascal, Josie?"

I lowered my head. "I wasn't invited."

"Pascal, Josie will go with you," Helen told our French friend.

"I didn't say that," I said.

Helen was annoyed. "Why won't you go? You're being rude."

"I'm being rude?" I asked. I probably shouldn't have said that.

Helen appealed to Tom. "Wouldn't you like some time alone with me?" she asked. Talk about putting a guy on the spot.

"Well . . ." Tom said in his most helpful manner.

Helen suddenly froze. "Pascal, why do you have to go back to work?"

"I have to go," he said.

"But why did you leave in the first place?" Helen insisted.

Tom could see where her questions were leading and tried to head her off. "I wanted him to have dinner with me. Pascal works late but gets a break at this time."

Pascal nodded. "We wanted dinner with you."

Helen caught the slip. "With *us?* You knew we would be here?"

"We were just walking by," Tom said.

Helen sat back and threw me an icy glance. "I don't believe any of this," she said. "Josie rests and reads to a certain hour and then suddenly she is starving and we have to hurry out to eat. Pascal, you knew we'd be here, didn't you?"

The young Frenchman wasn't able to follow every word Helen had uttered, but he could sense there was trouble. He adopted what he thought was a safe response. "It's been nice to see you, Helen," he said. "Goodbye." He got away fast, God bless his good sense.

Now there were just the three of us, two babes and a boy, an unstable formula if ever there was one. Helen continued to nod as if Pascal had confirmed her suspicions. Her sunburned skin turned an even deeper crimson. Humiliation, anger—they came in the same shades of red.

"How come you didn't tell me you talked to Tom today, Josie?" she asked.

"I didn't talk to him," I said smooth as silk, but Helen didn't believe me.

She ignored me for a moment and stared Tom in the eye. "Do you like Josie better than me?"

He shrugged. "I like both of you."

Her lower lip trembled. "Please just tell me the truth, Tom. That's all I ask."

I couldn't let him be raked over like that. There was no stopping Helen when she got like this. "I set this up," I admitted. "I did see Tom this afternoon."

Helen had known, sure, but now she *knew,* which was worse. She pounded the table with her fists, and our empty wine bottles danced.

"You just said you didn't!" she shrieked.

"I lied," I said. "I'm sorry. I told Tom to lie to you. I told him to bring Pascal so that Pascal would take you away and I could be with Tom. Everything that has happened is completely my fault. Tom had nothing to do with any of it. I twisted his arm."

My words had a strange effect on Helen. Rather than cause her to explode more, she grew quiet. Too quiet. It was a deadly calm. She ignored Tom and turned her attention on me. Her next question caught me like a slap in the face.

"Do you know that Ralph is dead?" she asked.

I couldn't speak for a moment. "No."

She nodded. "He died of natural causes soon after he moved away. I spoke to his mother, who told me. I thought her phrase 'natural causes' sounded odd. I mean, calling something that killed your only child 'natural.' Do you know what I mean, Josie?"

I swallowed, shocked. "Why didn't you tell me?"

"You didn't deserve to know." She stood up and regarded the two of us as if we were matching piles of vomit. "You two deserve each other." She nodded again, started to add something, but then must have thought better of it. She turned and disappeared in the same direction as Pascal. Tom and I looked at each other across the table, and I was grateful when he didn't say "I told you so."

"The night can only improve," Tom said instead.

I thought of Helen's previous suicide attempt. Yet, strange as it may sound, I wasn't in the least concerned that she'd make another attempt. She was a different girl from the one last summer. The gods had spoken to her. She was strong. She'd want revenge, not condolences. Not for one moment did I consider going after her.

"I wonder," I said.

CHAPTER 6

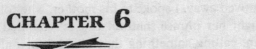

AN HOUR LATER TOM AND I WERE IN A SMALL BOAT DRIFT-
ing in Hora harbor beneath a huge moon. There was a
slight wind blowing, and the boat rocked with small
waves, but I felt safe. Our wooden vessel was only six
feet long. Tom and I sat facing each other, my
outstretched legs resting beside his. We had been
talking about something interesting, but silence had
fallen and was stretching to the point where I had to
wonder *when he would kiss me.*

The boat belonged to Pascal's boss. Apparently
Tom and Pascal were free to use it whenever they
wished. It had been pulled up on the beach and
chained down. I had helped Tom push it into the
water.

"So," I said, finally breaking the silence with the
stupidest question I could muster, "what do you think
of those Dodgers?"

"Is that a football team?" Tom asked.

"No. They prefer baseball. They can't take the hits."

"Do you like sports?"

I shrugged, and the boat shook with my movement. "I like to play any sport, but I could care less about organized teams." The harbor area at night, seen from the water, looked like an amusement park. The many lights reflected back on the sea. There were small choppy waves now and foam. The wind had picked up in the last *twenty* seconds. Interesting, I thought. We had drifted beyond the confines of the harbor and were beginning to feel the tug of the ocean currents. Tom acted unconcerned—so I did as well.

"You never told me what had brought you to Greece," Tom said.

"Helen."

He paused, as if he wished I hadn't told him. "Last time she was here she was obsessed with Delos," he said.

"You mentioned that. Did she really go every day?"

He nodded. "She came back every day with a horrible sunburn. I told her to use a screen, but she said she was. Anyway, she was always climbing to the top of Kynthos and lying out on the stones."

"That's where Apollo was supposed to have been born."

"No," Tom said. "On the summit of Kynthos are the ruined sanctuaries of Zeus and Athena. Apollo was worshiped on other parts of the island."

"Maybe Helen knows something we don't," I said. "But she was sure right about the power emanating from that place. It almost made my hair stand on end. I assume she tried to get you to go there?"

"She never asked me to go with her. But I had already been to Delos." He was curious. "You felt something there?"

"Oh, yes. It was incredible—a surge of peace and power."

"You're the first person who's ever said that," Tom said.

"I'm surprised. I wasn't imagining it."

"You must be sensitive, Josie."

I chuckled. "I'm about as sensitive as an L.A. city bench."

He laughed. "Are you still feeling guilty about what happened tonight?"

"Yeah. But I'd like to feel more guilty."

"What do you mean?"

I grinned mischievously. I wondered if he could see my expression in the moonlight. "I wish I had more to feel guilty about," I said.

He took the hint. He leaned forward to kiss me. In doing so he accidentally bumped our only oar and knocked it into the water. He went to grab it just as I shot forward to kiss him. The peck surprised him and he gave a start, laughing.

"Hey, that tickles," he said.

I kissed his cheek, adding a little bite. The moon

had that affect on me. I wanted to jump his bones. Yeah, sure, I know, blame it on the moon.

"Is that all it does?" I asked wickedly.

He fended me off. "Let me get this paddle, Josie, or we'll be—" He stopped, staring over the side of the boat. "Damn."

I followed his gaze. We were now clearly out of the harbor. In the space of two minutes the waves had grown to almost two feet, and the water was really churning. The wind—it was truly amazing—was suddenly blowing hard. I had to wipe the hair from my eyes to see clearly.

"The meltémi—it blows fiercely when the gods are in the mood."

The gods must have been in a humorous mood.

The oar was ten feet from the boat already.

"What should we do?" I asked.

"We have to retrieve it before it gets any farther away. We won't make it back in without it. We'll have to lean over the side and paddle with our arms. Let's do it quickly before we lose sight of the oar."

We tried his plan. It didn't work. The boat plowed in circles. Our hand paddles were uncoordinated. Tom told me to stop after a minute. He looked worried. The oar was an easy thirty feet away now and moving fast.

"What should we do?" I asked anxiously. I didn't want to drift out to sea, even if it was with Tom. The exotic blue of the Mediterranean was a different matter at night, especially with that damn wind blowing. The boat rocked precariously. Tom pulled off his shirt.

"I have to go after it," he said.

I grabbed his arm. "No. You'll drown."

He shook me off. "We have to head back to dock now. The current is pulling us out. We can't fight it without that oar."

I couldn't believe what was happening. I was wrong about the gods being in a funny mood. There was something almost malicious in the way the wind had come up. Tom kicked off his sandals and prepared to dive in.

"I'll be back in a few seconds," he promised.

I was staring over the side. "Where's the oar? I don't see it anymore, Tom."

He paused. The water was like angry gray soup being brought to a quick boil. All we were missing was the steam. Tom leaned forward and peered out.

"I can't see it either," he said.

"How can you swim for it if you don't know where it is?" I asked.

"I'll swim in that direction," he said, pointing. "I'll find it. I must go. Goodbye, Josie."

"Don't say that word." I gave him a quick hug. "Good luck."

Tom dove over the side. The ocean seemed to swallow him. It was several seconds before I caught sight of his head. His arms flailed in the moonlit cauldron. I think by going underwater and then coming up, he had disoriented himself. It didn't seem to me that he was swimming in the direction we had last observed the paddle. And all this, I thought, because I'd had to kiss him.

I shouted. "Tom! Go that way! That way! Not that way!"

He couldn't hear me. He must have had water in his ears, and now the wind was howling. The tiny boat twisted this way and that. Tom glanced back once—I think he was trying to orient himself using the boat, another mistake. Then he set off in a direction that I believed the oar had not floated.

Then he was gone.

Time passed.

Minutes, slowly bubbling, like the last breath of a man cast into the sea with cement for shoes. Bubbles of wasted time.

He was gone.

It was true.

I couldn't believe it.

"Tom!" I screamed. "Tom!"

I thought he might have been close but unable to see the boat.

"Tom!"

I screamed till I was hoarse.

Tom was gone. The sea had swallowed him up.

I hugged the sides of the boat, trying to keep it from toppling. Salt water splashed my face, stinging with the salt of the deep and the bitterness of my tears. I had not cried in a long time, since I had heard Helen had tried to take her life. Helen should have been with me then. She could have asked about the pain in my chest. It was as if a stone fist had been rammed through my sternum. I kept thinking the same thought over and over—it wouldn't go away.

Tom must have drowned by now.

Dead.

"Tom," I whispered.

Hora fell away. The lights, the partying, the people —they could have dropped into a black hole. Only it was me who was falling.

The current pulled me out to sea.

The *meltémi*. I didn't know what the word meant. If only I had a Greek scholar with me to consult. Girl, there are numerous definitions for *meltémi*. Nasty wind. Hard wind. No-sense-of-timing wind. Screw-you-Josie wind. You're-going-to-die wind.

Was I going to die? I thought that I might. The boat was riding as if on a roller coaster. I had to keep shifting my weight to counteract the instability caused by each slap of water. The waves were now hitting from every direction, and it was hard to keep up with them. Plus the farther I drifted from Mykonos, the higher the waves grew. When they were up to four feet they began to crash over the sides of the boat, and I had to bail furiously, using my hands as a cup. I tired quickly and I realized the sea had all night to claim me as a victim. I was mortal. In that moment the sea became a monster that could never be defeated by something living.

Mykonos fell behind me at remarkable speed. But I was not being dragged straight out from it; rather I was heading northwest, roughly on the same route the boat I had taken that morning. It was true, I was floating in the direction of Delos. That gave me cause for hope. If I washed up on shore, before my boat toppled, I would live. But if I missed the island, I was probably doomed.

I bailed faster, fighting my fatigue. I had a goal—stay afloat until Delos saved me. In my heart, I imagined the island as a mother who would embrace me, her child, in this time of great danger. The dream of a desperate soul, perhaps, but it gave me strength.

There was a problem with my bailing the water out of the boat, though. It required both hands, and I wasn't able to grip the gunwales. A cruel wave came from behind and caught me totally unprepared. I felt a sharp thump first and then suddenly I was toppling through the air. When I hit the water head-first, I almost let out a scream of pure terror. But had I done that, I would have let the sea into my lungs and drowned right then.

Maybe it would have been better to have let it end then.

Before the horrors that were to come.

I wonder still about many things.

I didn't scream. I fought to the surface and frantically searched for the boat, half blind with my hair plastered over my face. Silently, in my heart, I cursed Poseidon, the god of the sea, for doing this to me. Then, out of the blue—I should say out of the black—the boat hit me on the side of the head.

The boat was right side up, for which I was grateful, but it was rapidly filling with water. In a calm sea it would have been a cinch to climb into the small boat, but now my attempts to make it in only got me hit in the face by the wooden hull. Still, I clung to the boat as I had never held on to anything in my life. It was all I had left in the vast dark watery grave that my world had become.

After a few minutes I realized that part of the reason I couldn't climb back into the boat was bad timing. The waves kept knocking me back. I decided to take the waves' lead and follow them. I reasoned that if I could yank myself up just as a wave swelled behind me, the water should give me the extra lift I needed.

Looking over my shoulder, I followed a particularly large swell as it approached. Just before it hit, I pulled down on the gunwale of the boat with all my strength and kicked up with my right leg, as if I were attempting to clear a high-jump bar. It worked. The swell shoved up on my bottom, and I literally toppled into the boat, as if I had been thrown.

I was safe, for the moment.

There was no time to rest. I had to start bailing again and risk getting tossed over again. A minute into the chore another thought occurred to me. I was sitting facing the bow, as most anyone automatically would. Maybe, I decided, I should turn ninety degrees and face the side so I was able to brace my feet against one gunwale with my back against the other. This stabilized my position somewhat while leaving my hands free to bail.

"I'm not going overboard again," I swore under my breath.

I don't know how long all this took. It may have only been an hour, maybe three. Finally, though, I reached the point of exhaustion that defied all strength of will. My arms were cramped in knots that transformed them into useless sticks. My chest was a burning furnace of pain. The muscles in my back felt as if they were tearing every time I reached down to scoop out another handful of water. I had to stop. I slumped forward and cried on my trembling knees—I couldn't stop crying. I knew then that I was going to die.

"God," I whispered. "Where is my God?"

The wind. The waves. The pain.

Miracles are often tied to prayers.

Suddenly everything began to settle down.

God.

The *meltémi* was being reined in. As miraculously as it had hit, it vanished. The wind didn't merely slow, it stopped. In the space of five minutes the sea became as calm as a mountain lake just before the hand of winter closed its grip and the water froze. The silver rays of the moon shone on the flat surface with such mirror perfection that it was easy to imagine I was adrift in a sea of ice. I didn't know what to do—so I wept.

"My God," I cried softly over and over again.

I was so weary.

I lay down and slept.

CHAPTER 7

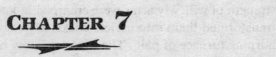

I AWOKE TO THE SOUND OF WATER GURGLING OVER POL-
ished stones. My eyes popped open and I sat up in an
instant. I thought I might find myself in my bed,
having survived nothing more than a terrifying
dream.

But I was still in the boat, soaking wet. Something
major had changed in the life-and-death struggle of
Josie, though. I was not lost in the middle of the
ocean. I had come aground on an island. I peered back
across the water, the way I had come, and believed I
saw the western tip of Mykonos, twinkling with the
yellow lights of civilization across the silver sheen of
the silent sea.

"Delos," I whispered. "She saved me."

I was ninety percent sure I had come aground on the
sacred island. I'd know in a few minutes. I climbed
out of the boat, glad to have solid earth beneath me.

Delos was small, and I had walked around half of it not that many hours before. In the moonlight I would easily be able to spot the ruins, once I got to higher ground.

I reasoned that I had come ashore on the southeastern end of the island, "the back" of it relative to where we had stepped ashore earlier that morning. A tall hill loomed overhead as I walked on rubbery legs along the rocky shore. Probably the pinnacle of Kynthos, I thought. Well, I had no intention of climbing it in the shape I was in, especially not just to get my bearings. A few hundred yards north, I thought, and the hills would be lower. Then I would be able to climb over to the ruins and knock at the door of the archaeologists. The pamphlet said no one lived on the island, but I had seen houses near the museum for the archaeological staff. I was anxious to call my father. He may have begun searching for me already. My watch had fallen off, and I had no idea what time it was.

For Tom, I held out little hope. But it was possible —just possible, I told myself—that he had been able to swim to shore. I clung to the hope to warm my shivering body.

The hill above me eventually dropped down and I turned inland. Miraculously—it was a night of miracles—I still had my sandals on. Nevertheless, I moved cautiously between shadows on the stony ground. Here there were tumbleweeds, sometimes rows of them that were difficult to circumvent, and soon my legs were scratched. Yet I almost welcomed the touch of the weeds because—

They belonged to Delos.

Yes, the farther I walked, the more I left behind the sea that had almost killed me, the more love I felt for the island. People would laugh if I told them *she* had saved me—Delos, the wandering star that shone in the night. I fantasized that Delos had moved while I slept in my tiny boat, a few feet, maybe a few hundred yards, to be sure to catch me before I drifted out to sea. Earlier, on my first visit to Delos, I had felt the unspoken welcome of the island. Now I experienced its actual embrace.

I crested the hill and looked down at the ruins in the moonlight.

The city was new.

I blinked. Nothing changed, although everything already had.

The city was alive.

People, beautiful creatures in long colored robes, walked among pillared walkways and sat upon marble chairs. Their long hair, gold and black and red, hung like shawls over their shoulders. They moved as if in a dream, or perhaps it was because I was in a dreamlike state. For I could not say how I felt at that moment. I should have been in shock. But I didn't register what I saw as real because I no longer felt human. I moved forward, toward them, wanting to be a part of them. Yet it was as if my feet no longer touched the ground. They floated and I drifted. I could vanish into space in an instant. It was good. I was in the right place at the right time. I was coming home to a place beyond space and time. A portion of my mind left me then, and a larger part of my soul entered the void.

I was whole again.

I was who I was.

I stepped into the city. The light was all around, the life of another time, the ancient Greeks, older even, much older, than the historians realized. The city was intoxicated. There was celebration; there was worship. There was an understanding that the gods were real, and could be pleased and give great fortune. I considered it my great fortune to enter the star of Delos.

I sat down on a smooth white seat.

Someone noticed me. Then another. They smiled joyfully, hopefully.

I closed my eyes and waited for them to come to me. To serve me.

CHAPTER 8

SRYOPE WAS THE DAUGHTER OF THALIA, MUSE OF APOLLO, but her father was unknown. When Sryope was young she would inquire of her mother how she came to be without a father, and Thalia would only answer, "It's a mystery." As Sryope grew, she quickly gained reknown as Thalia's equal in composing prose and poetry. Often Sryope was invited to Olympus to entertain the immortals. But by the time she came of age, Olympus was already in decline. Zeus, Hera, Athena, and Ares had departed for places unknown. It was Apollo who now ruled, but he was seldom ever seen, and no one knew where he spent his time. Yet when Sryope came to Olympus, it sometimes happened that Apollo would appear to listen to her enchanted tales. She had a lovely, mesmerizing voice.

Sryope's best friend was Phthia, daughter of Tyche, who was the daughter of Zeus. Phthia often spoke of her relationship to Zeus with pride, although she could not say who *her* own father was. In that way Sryope and Phthia were the same. Many said they had been born on the same day at the same time, although Thalia, Sryope's mother, said this was not so. In either case Sryope and Phthia grew up together and were best friends. Sryope would tell stories and Phthia would play her flute, which had been a gift to her from Pan, the only immortal who was known to have been killed.

It came to pass that a child was born to Aphrodite, the goddess of beauty. The child was called Aeneas, and his father was known to have been a mortal, much to Aphrodite's shame. It seemed that Aphrodite was not immune to her own magic girdle, which could cause anyone to fall in love. But Aeneas grew up well and was prized by the gods because of his extreme beauty and exquisite manners.

Phthia was the first female to capture Aeneas's attention as he entered manhood. Aeneas was fond of swimming the rivers that flowed behind the temples of Olympus, and Phthia knew of this habit and made it a point to be in the rivers at the same time, but naked, so that Aeneas would lust for her and make her his wife. Now, Phthia was well known for her many lovers, but she had never wanted a god as much as she wanted Aeneas. This she told to Sryope, who could understand Phthia's infatuation because she, too, found Aeneas attractive. But Sryope didn't speak a word of this attraction to Phthia, who was known to have a temper.

Now Aeneas, when he spied Phthia naked in the waters beside him, was consumed with lust, for she was very beautiful. Aeneas was unaware of her reputation as a seducer, and he gave himself over to her, and she to him, after she first made him promise that he would love her, and no other, as long as Olympus stood. This Aeneas readily agreed to because he was dizzy with passion. So Aeneas and Phthia were together for some time.

But it came to pass that Phthia soon tired of loving Aeneas exclusively and began to entertain other suitors. This Aeneas learned from Sryope, who told Aeneas that Phthia had always been this way and always would be. Sryope told Aeneas to leave Phthia and come with her, for by this time Sryope was much in love with Aeneas, having watched from afar as he pleased Phthia with his amorous ways. But Aeneas was heartbroken that Phthia had lied to him about her fidelity. He explained to Sryope that he could not leave Phthia, no matter what she did, because of the vow he had sworn to her. Sryope was not easily put off.

"It is Phthia who made you swear the vow," Sryope said. "It is Phthia who can release you from the vow."

"But she will never do so," Aeneas said. "Her jealousy is well known."

"I know it well myself," Sryope said. "Nevertheless, Phthia must release you from your vow, and I will force her to do so."

Sryope thought about the matter and eventually came up with a plan that she told to Aeneas, who was by this time eager to be free of Phthia.

At the heart of Sryope's scheme was her knowledge of who Phthia's father was. It had come to Sryope in a vision while she worshiped Apollo. Visions were common with Sryope. Indeed, her greatest stories came from trances she entered while she was in the rapture of worship. It was Sryope's belief that the sun itself, the life-giver of all the realms, human and divine, sometimes spoke through her. But this was a secret she kept from everyone, lest she invoke the wrath of the other gods. For the gods as a group were notoriously jealous of one another, with few exceptions. It was a disease of character that had spread through Olympus as the centuries passed.

Phthia's father, Sryope knew, was Alecto, of the realm of Hades, one of the three Furies who was responsible for listening to the complaints brought by mortals against one another and who was also responsible for punishing mortals. The three Furies were horrible. They usually were shaped as crones, with snakes for hair, dog's heads, coal-black bodies, bat's wings, and bloodshot eyes. But because they were older than Zeus, their powers were a mystery. It was also said they could assume beautiful forms when it suited them.

It happened long ago that Alecto, whom some said was the strongest of the Furies, had become angered by Zeus because he had lightened the punishment of mortals Alecto had decreed should suffer horrible

CHRISTOPHER PIKE

deaths. As a means of revenge, Alecto changed herself into a handsome warrior and stole into the bed of Tyche, Zeus's daughter, while she lay sleeping. Feeling the touch of a warrior on her naked limbs, Tyche awoke and made passionate love to the Fury. When they were done Alecto cast off her disguise and told Tyche that she was now pregnant with the daughter of a Fury.

"Now there is no telling what will happen," Alecto said. "You being, O Tyche, the goddess of fortune for all mortals everywhere. This child will not leave you for a long time, and her life will constantly affect your judgment of what mortals should receive and what they should be denied."

Horrified by the prophecy, Tyche fled to her father, Zeus, to explain to him what had happened. At the news Zeus was angered, and even though he was then king of Olympus, he was loath to try to directly challenge the curse of a Fury. But he did decide to try to postpone the effect of the curse by lengthening the gestation period of Tyche's child, from nine months to ninety thousand.

"That way," Zeus explained, "the child will not arrive until Olympus and the Earth are much changed."

But Tyche was still fearful. "But my child will still be the daughter of a Fury and will most likely be hideous."

Zeus shook his head. "I can make it so that the child is born beautiful and talented. Indeed, even of a pleasant disposition and manner. Is this what you

108

wish, Daughter? Then the true nature of the child will be harder for others to detect. As a goddess of beauty, the child might cause even more trouble."

But Tyche wanted it so, and she made Zeus promise that no one should know who was the father of the child. To this Zeus reluctantly agreed.

So in her vision, which even Zeus could not shield, Sryope saw the full tale of Phthia's origin, and it made her laugh and cry at the same time. Because Phthia was her friend, they had spent much of their lives together. But the pride Phthia took in being Zeus's granddaughter had always annoyed Sryope, and now that they were rivals for the love of Aeneas, it annoyed her even more.

Sryope went to Phthia and confronted her with the truth, which made Phthia laugh at her. But Sryope said, "Go to your mother and ask her if I don't speak the truth. As you know, your mother can never lie."

So Phthia went to her mother and asked her to condemn Sryope's vicious gossip, but Tyche did not respond. Tyche could not lie, but she could remain silent when the truth was too painful to reveal. This Phthia knew, and she realized with horror that what Sryope said was true, that she was the daughter of a Fury. Phthia hurried back to Sryope and asked her to swear that she would never reveal this fact to anyone. Sryope agreed, but on one condition.

"You have to challenge me to a contest on Mt. Olympus," Sryope said. "A contest to see who can tell the best story. If you win, I swear to keep the truth of your father secret. But if I win you must give up all claim to Aeneas, and free him from the vow of fidelity that he swore to you."

To these terms Phthia happily agreed because she secretly thought that Sryope could have forced her to give up Aeneas without a contest. Sryope was a reknowned storyteller, but Phthia, displaying the inflated ego inherent in being the descendant of a Fury, actually believed that she could defeat Sryope. She said this aloud to herself.

"I will tell a tale that shames her finest story," Phthia said. "Then all the fair gods of Olympus will long for my love. And I will keep Aeneas bound to his vow to repay him for wanting to consort with Sryope behind my back."

Word of the contest spread throughout the realm, and on the appointed day all the gods gathered on Olympus to hear who would weave the more captivating story. Apollo himself consented to come. He sat on the throne that had once belonged to Zeus and nodded that the contest should begin. Sryope asked to go first, and this also pleased Phthia, because she thought it easier to make the stronger impression after her childhood friend had spoken.

But Sryope did not intend to give Phthia a chance to speak. She had promised Phthia that, whether she won or lost the contest, she would tell no one of how the Fury had seduced Tyche and given life to Phthia. But Sryope had not promised not to retell the actual story by changing the names and a few of the details so that the unenlightened would not know it was based on truth.

This was what Sryope did. She told the assembly of gods the tale of Phthia's heritage, but she did it in such a way that she could never be accused of breaking her promise to Phthia.

At first the gods didn't know that Sryope's story was anything but a product of her wonderful imagination. But as Sryope continued, and Phthia began to tremble, and then to weep, a stir went through the crowd. Phthia was her own worst enemy that day. If she had managed to keep silent, the gods would have assumed she was upset because Sryope's story was so wonderful it was unbeatable. But Phthia mistakenly believed everyone must know the story was about her. Also, her hatred for Sryope in that moment was so great that she could not control herself. A Fury's anger could never be reined in once it was let loose.

Phthia leapt up when Sryope was almost finished. She swore at her childhood friend. "You promised you would not talk about me!"

Sryope feigned innocence. "Am I talking about you, Phthia? The goddess in my story is named Dene. How could you be connected to a Fury? Surely you are confused. You cannot be the daughter of one of those demons."

At that Phthia stepped close to Sryope and spoke so that only she could hear. "You know that I am descended from a demon. But you don't know what kind of demon I am. You will know and soon, Sryope, that I promise you. You will loath the day you ever met me."

With that Phthia fled from Mt. Olympus and was

not seen ever again. The assembly of gods scattered, and for a long time there was much talk of the contest between the two old friends, Sryope and Phthia. But no one knew what Phthia had said to Sryope just before she vanished, and no one was ever sure that Phthia was the daughter of a Fury. It didn't seem likely, most of the gods said. The Furies were awful beyond measure and Phthia had been a good goddess, although extremely promiscuous. That in itself was not considered a fault for a goddess, most believed.

Aeneas came to be Sryope's husband, and the two lived in peace for many years. Sryope continued to entertain the gods with her stories, but she soon began to spend more time on Earth, giving stories to human writers and poets in dreams and visions. This she did gladly, for it seemed to her mortals appreciated the tales even more than her fellow gods, and they learned from them to be brave and generous, and kind and noble. But Sryope had trouble conveying stories that embodied truth because she herself had deceived Phthia, although in a clever way.

The gods did not appreciate her giving so many of her talents to mortals. They were jealous of her gifts, which they considered belonged to them alone. But to this feeling Sryope paid no heed and lengthened her stays on Earth, where things were changing fast, as Zeus had long ago predicted they would.

Sryope was on Earth, walking the shore of one of the mortals' vast oceans at night, when the three Furies came for her with their whips and chains. They appeared before her as a whirling cloud of blood and dirt. Before she could flee, a thorny noose was thrown over her neck and she was thrown to the ground. Tisiphone, Megaera, and terrible Alecto stood over her, feverish, as if in anticipation of a human sacrifice —their greatest joy. Though frightened, Sryope swore that Apollo would have their heads for attacking her in this fashion. At this Alecto laughed and stepped forward.

"It is Apollo," Alecto said, "who sent us to arrest you and bring you to trial on Mt. Olympus."

"I am to be brought to trial?" Sryope asked, confused. "But I have done nothing wrong."

Alecto stopped laughing and spit on Sryope, the saliva the color of a human's blood. "You have murdered Phthia. Don't deny it. You have hated her since you were young. Her lifeless body has been found floating in the River Styx."

"But the Styx runs through the Underworld," Sryope protested. "Only mortals go that way when they die, not gods. Phthia was an immortal and could not die anyway."

Alecto pulled Sryope to her feet by her hair and chained her arms and legs. "That is true," the crone said. "But nevertheless she did die, and it is you who sent her that way. For that crime, proud muse of the mortals, you will pay dearly."

CHAPTER 9

I AWOKE AT DAWN IN THE RUINS OF DELOS. I WAS LYING propped up against an overturned pillar of chipped marble. All around me was the erosion of centuries. My vision of the night before, of a city magically reborn from the past, was gone. I was alone and I was cold.

Yet I had the memory of my dream of Sryope still with me, and it was enough to make my blood pound. I didn't know what any of it meant. I had no idea what was happening in my life. I wondered, briefly, if I was not losing my mind.

Especially when I saw the artifact standing on the low pillar beside me. It was a tiny marble statue of a goddess, about five inches tall. Rolling onto my knees, I reached over and picked it up. For an instant I felt the same magnetic current I had when I had leaned against one of the main supports of Apollo's temple. It

114

went up my arm and into my head before stopping. The details of the face were few, but I was not misled.

"Sryope," I whispered.

I was holding a statue of the goddess in my dream. Of all the things I could see around me in Delos, it was the only one that was not ruined by time. I didn't know where it had come from. I didn't know what to do with it. But I couldn't very well leave it for someone else to take. I stuffed it in my pocket and stood up.

There was a bright glow in the east, in the direction of Mykonos. But I could not see the sun because I was on the west side of the hills of Delos, in reality, not far from the museum and the living quarters. The previous night it had been my intent to go straight to the archaeologists and have them call my father. But now I was wary. It was morning, and I had been on the island half the night. They would wonder why I hadn't come to them immediately. I knew of the government's extreme fear that anyone should take anything from the sacred island. Of course, I was not a thief. I had come to the island by chance. I had nothing to hide.

Except the statue. I didn't want to give them Sryope. She belonged to me—I was the one dreaming about her. If I went to the archaeologists they would search me as a precautionary measure before they let me go. There was no way I was going to let them do that.

My next choice was simple. I would hurry back to where I had come ashore, set the boat adrift, and hide out on the southeast side until the tourists arrived. Then I could mingle with them and go home with the crowd with my goddess in my pocket.

I set off, back the way I had come during the night.

I didn't stop to ask myself why I was so anxious to hold on to my trophy. Certainly I wasn't thinking of stealing her for the purpose of trying to sell her. I just liked her, and—here I was showing definite signs of insanity—I thought she liked me, too.

The archaeologists, and whatever security Delos possessed, must have slept late. I got out of the main area of the ruins without difficulty. The hills were no obstacle for a girl who had beaten Poseidon, god of the seas, at his own game. The brand-new sun stung my eyes as I crested the stony summit. Kynthos shone orange on my right, and I almost paused to salute Apollo's birthplace. That the god had been born there, I no longer had any doubt, although I had no reason to believe Helen over Tom.

Tom.

The thought of him came to me then. But I refused to feel grief until I was sure he was dead. There was a chance, I told myself over and over, that he had made it to shore. He had clearly been a strong swimmer.

I made my way down to the shore and headed to the right, south, walking with my sandals splashing in the water. When I reached the spot where I was certain I had come ashore, I found my boat gone. I wasn't surprised. While I slept, the tide could easily have carried it back out to sea. Actually, the boat's not being there made my job easier because I had no intention of telling whoever was looking for me that I had spent the night on Delos. I had no desire to tell *anybody,* including my father, what I had seen there.

I sat down and rested. The walking had warmed me, and now, on this side of the island, with the sun shining on me, I was comfortable. I estimated the time at six o'clock. The first tourists would arrive at about eight-thirty. Then I would be able to go over to the snack bar and get a cup of coffee and a Danish. The thought was divine.

My plan went as I envisioned, except I waited till nine before sneaking over the hill and joining the scurrying visitors, who could have been from all appearances the same group that had come to Delos the previous day. No one gave me a second look, although my green shorts and white top looked as if they had been put through a night of homelessness.

The snack bar was open and waiting for me. It was a shame that I hadn't a penny with me. Fortunately, the young Greek man at the counter recognized me from the day before and took pity on me and gave me coffee and a roll for free after I explained to him that I was broke. As I sat down, I thought about how Helen was wrong about the Greek people. They were gracious hosts.

After leaving the snack bar, I loitered around the

museum. There was a mural on the wall that reminded me slightly of Sryope, but the artist had made her slightly masculine. I strolled around with my hands in my pockets so no one would realize I had something in them.

I didn't hike back to the top of Kythnos. I was tired and had had enough mystical experiences to last me for one vacation.

In reality, I truly did believe something odd might happen to me on Kythnos. For the time being I preferred to believe what was happening to me was a trauma-induced hallucination. There was logic in that.

But it didn't explain away the artifact I carried.

Where had it come from?

It was almost as if someone had left it for me to find while I slept.

But why?

I ran into a small hitch when I went to leave. By then it was noon and the second boat was docked at Delos. A man stood near the boarding ramp of the first boat checking the payment slips so that, I suppose, someone could not leave early on a boat they hadn't come over on. But I just smiled sweetly and told the guy I had lost my slip, and I was waved through.

The ride back to Mykonos took the usual twenty-five minutes, but it seemed an eternity. As we entered the harbor of Hora, I was glad to see my father and Silk standing on the dock. Regrettably, they were talking to what looked like two police officers. I couldn't get off the boat fast enough to show my dad I was alive. The poor man, I thought, how he must have suffered since he learned I was gone.

The big boat was finally secured. I ran down the gangplank. But then I realized my folly. I had to act like nothing was amiss. I slowed my steps and strolled up to my father and Silk and gave them a carefree smile.

"Hi," I said.

My father—God bless his heart—burst out crying. He wrapped me in a huge hug. Even Silk appeared happy to see me, and that was a definite first. The two police officers stood watching and no doubt wondering if I was another one of those filthy—flaky—Americans. Finally my dad let me go. I put on a face like he was overreacting just a tad, although I felt like crying myself.

"Where have you been?" he asked.

I shrugged. "I went to visit Delos again. Why? You all look upset."

In reality he had never looked happier in his life. "We thought you were dead," he said. "Tom told us that—"

"Tom!" I screamed. So much for my casual act. I grabbed my dad as hard as he had grabbed me. "He's alive?"

"Sure," my dad said, laughing, confused out of his gourd and not minding much because I at least was safe. "He's out on a search boat now, looking for you.

Half the island is doing the same. Helen's with Tom."
Dad glanced at the police. "This is my daughter. The
one we've been looking for."

They nodded, as if to say they had I.Q.s above fifty.

"How did Tom get back to shore?" I asked.

"He swam," Silk said. "How did you get back to
shore?"

I gestured over my shoulder. "I took the boat."

"I don't understand," my dad said. "Where did you
spend the night?"

"On the beach," I said, realizing my mistake.

"What beach?" Silk asked.

I pointed to a small sandy area off the main coast of
Hora. When we had been walking with the guys the
first night, on our way to the big ferry, I had noticed a
number of young people camping there.

"After Tom dived overboard after the oar," I explained, "I drifted way out. But then the current
changed and I came back in. By then it was the middle
of the night. The boat plowed up on the sand. I
climbed out and collapsed. I didn't wake up until the
horn blew at eight o'clock for the boat leaving to
Delos."

"But why did you go to Delos again?" my dad
asked. "Didn't you know that we'd be frantic searching for you?"

"I thought you said yesterday when we got back
from Delos that you were thinking of going again
today," I said.

My dad stopped. "I did say that, but I wasn't
serious. Also, of course I wouldn't return there with

you lost at sea." He was exasperated. "Josie! We've been up all night worried about you!"

"I'm sorry," I said. "I thought there was a chance you might be on the boat bound for Delos, and then when I got aboard and saw you weren't there, it was too late to get off." I hugged him again. "You must have had a horrible night."

"You can't imagine," he said.

Oh, but I could. But I didn't tell him that.

Tom was alive! That was all that mattered. It didn't even bother me that he was with Helen. He was searching for me, thinking of me. I was happy.

For a short time.

CHAPTER 10

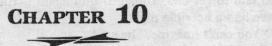

I RETURNED TO THE HOTEL TO REST. WHILE I WAS THERE MY father called off the search. Apparently he *had* hired many of the local fishermen to go out searching for me, in addition to the Greek authorities who were scouring the local islands. Fortunately most of them had radios on their boats and were able to return to dock promptly. The boat Helen and Tom were on was also notified. I could imagine Tom's relief—and, I assumed, Helen's. At the time I didn't know Pascal was also with them, that they were, in fact, on his boss's boat. This was the same boss who had lent Tom our boat the night before. All the attention I was receiving was wonderful, although it made me shudder to think what my mishap was costing my father.

Eventually the island police did come to the hotel to question me on where I had spent the night. I repeated the story I had told my father. They had only one difficulty with it. Where was the boat? I told them I had been too exhausted to secure it, that it must have been dragged back out to sea. I didn't know if they believed me or not—it was hard to read the body language of two men who had grown up in a different culture—but I'm sure they couldn't think of a reason why I'd lie to them. They left the hotel at about the same time as Helen, Pascal, and Tom arrived.

It was a joyous reunion. All three of them wouldn't let me off the hook for not contacting them the second I got back, but the complaints were made with big smiles. Helen in particular seemed relieved. In fact, she burst out crying when she first saw me. I decided I was forgiven for the previous night.

There may have been another reason than my return from the dead to account for Helen's warmth. Very quickly, as we were all talking and laughing together, I noticed that Helen and Pascal were standing close to each other. When I finally had Tom alone for a moment, I asked him about it.

"I noticed it on the boat on the way back, after we had learned you were safe," Tom said. "I think we lucked out and she fell for him. I know for a fact Pascal likes her." He grinned. "It takes the pressure off us, doesn't it?"

"Do you think we could spend time together alone without upsetting the situation?" I asked.

"She is your friend, but I'm sure it would be fine. Honestly, on the boat on the trip home, she let Pascal rub sunscreen on her back for an hour. She giggled half the time." Tom paused. "You know, I have this afternoon off. We could go to the other side of the island, and I could show you some beaches you probably haven't seen."

"Did you take the day off work because you thought I was dead?"

His face darkened. "I did think I would never see you again."

I nodded. "I thought the same thing."

When we rejoined Helen and Pascal, they were planning a barbecue for that evening. There were numerous barbecue pits on the beach in front of the hotel. All this partying to celebrate my resurrection. I told them I thought it sounded like a wonderful idea.

I had to work to get Helen alone for a minute. Her face was still streaked with dried tears, but her eyes glistened with a light I hadn't seen in ages.

"Do you hate me?" I asked.

She laughed. "I want to hate you, but I'm too happy you're alive." She hugged me again. "No, it's all water under the bridge, as they say."

I laughed. "I got plenty of water thrown in my face last night."

She let go of me, serious. "Were you scared?"

I was equally serious. "Yeah. I thought I would die."

"I didn't."

"I'm glad."

"No, I mean it, Josie. The whole time we were searching for you on the boat, I knew you were alive—somewhere. I could feel you still here."

"Thank you. I mean, I appreciate the sentiment." I took a breath. "I want to clear the air between us. You're my friend and I want you to remain my friend. If you don't want me to see Tom, if you feel like you saw him first and he belongs to you, then I won't talk to him anymore."

Helen was amused. "Do you mean that?"

"No, but I have to say it."

"Oh, Josie, you are sly."

"I hear I'm not the only one. Is it true about you and Pascal?"

"Is what true?" Helen asked.

"That you did it with Pascal on the boat while searching for my dead body?"

Helen waved her hand. "Four times. We couldn't help ourselves." She paused. "I like him."

"Pascal?"

"Yes. We're talking about the guy from France, not the one from England. I like him more than I liked Tom. Really, Josie, I'm happy this all happened the way it did. Everything's working out for the best. You and Tom go off and have fun." She added, "Just be back in time for the barbecue."

"Will you be at the barbecue?" I asked. Helen never ate beef.

Helen nodded. "Silk said she'd buy me chicken at the store. As long as I don't have to eat red meat, I'm happy."

Tom took me to a beach that he said wasn't on the map. I believed him—it was that small. A few yards of gold sand wedged between towering gray rocks. We had the whole place to ourselves. We had hardly dropped our towels when I, on impulse, pulled off my clothes, including my bathing suit, and ran into the water. I paused on the beach only long enough to see Tom's expression. Just the right combination of shock and lust, I thought.

Some people saw white light when they had a near-death experience; I saw my sexual prime slipping away.

Tom caught up with me in the water, and I was disappointed that he still had his swimming trunks on.

"Hey," I complained. "That's not fair."

"I can't take these off. I might jump on you if I did."

"I don't mind, honestly, Tom, I'm on vacation."

"But I don't have a condom. Safe sex, AIDS—politically correct, remember?"

I frowned. "Where does the politically correct come in?"

He shrugged, looking at my naked chest. We were standing in three feet of water. "They sure know how to grow them in California," he said.

I smiled, grabbing for his pants. "I want to see how they grow them at Oxford."

But he was too quick for me, diving underwater and swimming away. I couldn't believe the guy. Here I was stark naked, and he hadn't even kissed me yet.

"I know what it is!" I called after him. "You and Pascal are gay lovers!"

He resurfaced fifty feet out. "What?"

"Never mind." I turned and strode back to shore, calling over my shoulder, "Please look at my butt at least or I will think you don't care."

"I can't see without my contacts," he called.

"Oh boy," I whispered.

Tom eventually joined me on the beach, but by that time I had my bathing suit on. He looked disappointed.

"I was hoping to rub suntan lotion on your bare chest," he said.

I read my book and pretended to be bored. "I give a guy one chance, and if he doesn't take it I never forgive him."

Standing above me, he kicked the book out of my hand. "You can't read on a day like this with a guy like me with you."

I threw sand at him. "I've heard Oxford is nothing but a school for a bunch of nerdy bookworms."

He knelt beside me. "There is some truth to that statement. But this nerd could be changed, with one kiss, into a gentleman of heroic proportions." He leaned closer. I could actually feel his breath on my skin, cool compared to the heat of the sun. It was another glorious day on Mykonos. I think the Greek government manufactured them on the mainland and mailed them out each week on a plane. I was about to get my first kiss from the boy of my dreams. I laughed at him.

"You know what happened the last time we tried to kiss?" I asked.

He stopped. "I knocked the oar overboard." He

looked around. "What terrible calamity could befall us here if I made another attempt?"

"I might get pregnant."

"I can control myself."

"I can control you," I said. Then, in a sudden rush, I grabbed him and had him in my arms. He didn't know what had hit him. I smothered him in kisses. I ate him alive. I'm sure, without even straining my feminine charms, I could have had his trunks off in two seconds. But I wanted to give him just a taste, so that later, when I gave him the real thing, he would want to marry me. Ralph had asked me to marry him after we had had sex the first time.

In all the excitement, I had forgotten that Ralph was dead.

Just the thought was enough to curb my lust. I pulled aside.

"What's the matter?" Tom asked, blinking.

I smiled quickly. "Nothing. I was just thinking about politically correct behavior. You know, I'm fertile this time of the month."

"I can't say I knew that."

I smiled at him once more but felt the strain in the expression. "Tom, is there anything about me you find unusual?" I asked.

"If you take off your bikini again, I might be able to give you a better idea."

"I'm serious. Is there anything about me that you feel makes me different from other girls? I don't mean in a normal way."

He was puzzled. "Do you mean in a bad way?"

"No. I've been having weird experiences since I arrived on Mykonos." I glanced at my bag that held the statue of the goddess I had taken from Delos. I'd been afraid to leave it in my room in case Helen found it. No, it would be more accurate to say I had been reluctant to part from it.

Tom was concerned. "What kind of experiences? Have you been sick?"

"No, not sick. But I've been having strange dreams. Not only that, I've been having—visions."

"What kind of visions?"

"I didn't spend last night sleeping on the beach, Tom."

He wasn't surprised. "Were you on Delos?"

"Yes. How did you guess?"

"Because you came back from there this afternoon, and last night, when the wind came up, the current should have naturally taken the boat in that direction. Why didn't you tell us what really happened?"

"Because of what I saw when I was on the island. I know this will sound weird, but when the boat ran ashore on Delos and I climbed over to where the ruins were, I found the city as it was thousands of years ago."

"I don't understand."

I took his hand and lowered my head. "There were people there from the past. They were dressed in long robes and they walked among beautiful marble pillars. When I entered their city they recognized me. They wanted to serve me."

"You were having a dream."

I raised my head. "No, I had the dream afterward. In it I saw how the goddesses Sryope and Phthia fought over the handsome youth Aeneas."

Tom was watching intently. "You're upset, Josie."

I swallowed past a lump. "You're right. But I'm not crazy. After my dream, I woke up on Delos beside an ancient artifact." I reached for my bag. "The only thing is, this statue looks as new as the day it was made." I pulled out the goddess. "This is Sryope, Tom."

He stared at the work. "It's quite beautiful. You found this on Delos?"

"Yes. Wait!" He had started to take it. "You mustn't touch her."

He chuckled uncomfortably. "I'm not going to hurt her, Josie."

"No. But she can hurt you." The words were out of my mouth before I realized I had spoken them. I pulled the statue closer to my chest, to my heart, where I felt it belonged. "I don't understand this, Tom. I only know that you mustn't touch this thing. No one can."

He was patient with me, or else he was humoring me. "Where exactly did you find this on Delos?"

"It was standing beside me when I awoke from my strange dream."

"It wasn't there when you went to sleep?"

"No. The entire ancient civilization was there when I went to sleep."

"Josie—"

130

"Tom, it was. I saw it with my own eyes and I was not asleep."

"Was Delos in ruins when you left this afternoon?"

"Yes."

"What are you saying then? That you went back in time?"

"I don't know. All I know is that I am connected to that place in some way I can't explain. That it draws me to it, as it drew Helen last year."

"Have you talked to Helen about your strange experiences?"

"Not really."

"Why don't you talk to her?"

"No," I said suddenly. The strength of my reply gave him a start. I let go of his hand and clasped it instead to the lower portion of the statue. "She is the last person I want to talk to about these things."

"You don't trust her? She seems to be over her anger."

"It's not that," I said, although I may have been lying. "It's just one of those things that I have to bounce off someone objective. Helen's not objective." I gave a snort. "She's as crazy as I am."

"But you said you're not crazy, Josie."

I gestured weakly. "I am explaining this poorly. These dreams I'm having are not normal dreams. They are startling in their clarity. Plus I remember every bit of them when I wake up. Tom, are you familiar with the Furies in Greek mythology?"

"Yes. They are crones who live in the Underworld.

There are three of them. Offhand, I can't remember their names."

"Their names are Tisiphone, Megaera, and Alecto. Their jobs are to listen to the complaints mortals have against one another, and then to punish those that they think deserve it. Is that true?"

"Essentially."

"How did you know that, Tom?"

He shrugged. "I've made a casual study of Greek mythology."

"I haven't. I've never read about the Greek gods. I have never heard of the Furies before. But I dreamed about them on Delos last night, and I can tell you exactly what they look like. What do you think of that?"

"Somewhere you must have read about them, or seen a program on TV where they talked about the Furies. Greek mythology is popular worldwide."

"You're saying that consciously I didn't remember them, but my subconscious did and tucked them into my dream without my permission?"

"Yes."

"That's BS."

"It sounds a lot better than saying you spent the night on Mt. Olympus in your astral body."

"Tom, I am serious. How can you explain away this statue?"

He peered at it once more. "You definitely won't let me touch it?"

"No." I felt a wave of anxiety. I clasped the goddess

132

closer to my bosom. "I think it could kill you to touch it."

Tom took a deep breath. "What does it feel like it's made of?"

"Why, marble."

"It looks to me as if it has some kind of crystal mixed in with the marble," Tom said.

He was right. How odd, I thought, that I hadn't noticed before the numerous crystal chips blended into the tiny statue. It didn't seem like something I could have missed.

"They weren't there before," I muttered.

"Josie—"

"All right, I might have missed them. But you've got to admit this statue is remarkable. You can't buy something like this in town."

Tom was thoughtful. "It does look unusual. But you're never going to get it out of the country without an inspection of some kind."

"What do you mean?"

"The Greek people have lost thousands of precious archaeological objects over the last thirty years as a result of people finding them and taking them home. You have to accept the fact that someone will handle that statue eventually."

"I'll bury it in my luggage."

"They X-ray the bags. An object such as this will jump out at their trained eyes."

"But no one must touch Sryope." I caught myself, sounding mad even to myself. I put the statue back in my bag. "I will cross that hurdle when I come to it."

"What are you going to do now?"

"What do you think I should do?" I asked.

"Stay away from Delos. Stay out of small boats at night. Stay close to me."

I had to smile, he was so cute. I couldn't believe that I had moments before stripped naked in front of him. Really, I had just met him. He could have been an ax murderer for all I knew. I was worse than a promiscuous goddess, tempting the fates.

"To you?" I asked. "Is that wise?"

He reached over and took me in his arms. "Very wise," he said. "I'm your handsome youth Aeneas. I'm your god."

He kissed me—I let him. But my mood had shifted. My lust would have to wait. I suddenly knew that when I went to sleep that night I would have to witness Sryope's trial. I knew, too, that the verdict would be bitter.

"Don't be a god," I whispered in Tom's ear. "They don't have it so great."

CHAPTER 11

THE BARBECUE WAS GREAT. I WOULDN'T HAVE BELIEVED I could have so much fun, especially with Silk there. But she was playing the perfect mom, preparing the food and carrying it out to be roasted on the fiery iron bars of the charcoal-heated pit: hamburgers, lamb, breasts of chicken, onions—all marinated in some greasy sauce that smelled OK as long as you didn't get too close.

Helen helped Silk by turning over the meat with a long screwdriver—it was all we could find—but only when my dad shouted from the sidelines that it was time. Of course, no one would let me do any work because I was still supposed to be recovering from my trauma. Some recovery—I had spent half of it trying to get laid. Tom promised me that next time he brought me to his secluded beach—tomorrow—he would have condoms.

Pascal and Tom played Frisbee on the sand while they waited for the food. I hadn't known they had Frisbees in Europe.

Then we were all eating and talking and it was like the good old days, the ones that had really never been. I had *retsina* with my hamburger—I was developing a taste for it. I would probably be a drunk when I went home, I thought. Silk and I could go to AA meetings together and "connect" on that level. Yes, ladies and gentlemen, I now import ten cases of *retsina* a month and drink four bottles each day when the final bell at school rings. I am a recovering Mykonos enthusiast.

I cornered my dad during the meal. He remained seated near the pit, apparently enjoying the hot smoke blowing on his bare legs. Far out at sea, a swollen red sun played with purple clouds. It would soon set. The wind, though pleasant for the moment, was growing in strength. I had a fresh respect for the *meltémi* and didn't think I would stay out long. I hadn't exactly gotten my required eight hours the night before. I sat in the sand beside my father, still working on my first hamburger. I had ordered two but believed now that one would be it.

"I have more ideas for your story," I said.

My father smiled. His good humor over my rebirth was a thing that refused to go away. Everything I said made him smile. "You mean, our story," he said.

"We'll see. When we last left our hero, David

Herrick, and his alien captive, Vani, they were preparing to land on the alien home world. David had just learned from Vani that it was highly unlikely that a sweet woman like David's wife, Jessica, would have decided to leave a hero like David. Vani says David's superiors put her up to it and David is inclined to believe her. Is that all correct?"

"Yes," my dad said. "We were stuck with what happens when they land on the world."

"I know that part," I said quickly. "David, using Vani as a shield and guide, quickly plants the bomb and starts the detonation cycle. He has maybe thirty minutes until it goes off. Then, taking Vani with him, he blasts back off into space. Almost immediately he is surrounded by alien warships. They are ready to blow him out of space when he tells them about the bomb."

"Go on," my dad said.

"David tells the aliens that he is transmitting a coded sequence of numbers to his bomb and that if he stops it will explode. This could be true, by the way. He could be delaying the detonation of the bomb with his transmission. David tells the aliens that they have to let him go or he will blow up their world. Obviously, David has rigged it so that if they try to move the bomb it will automatically explode. He explains this to them as well."

"Go on," my dad said.

"They have to let him go but they can't let him go. They can't trust him to hand over the code once he is gone, so they are in a dilemma. But so is David. For all intents and purposes, he has been captured by the aliens."

"This is good," my dad said. "Do you have more?"

"Just one last thing. During this time, during this standoff, Vani struggles desperately to tell David something. But this something is one of those key points David's superiors have brainwashed her not to talk about. Like you said, she has the pain implants in her brain, and every time she tries to get the words out, she is struck down by waves of intolerable agony."

"What is she trying to tell him?" my dad asked.

"I don't know," I said. "I'm sorry."

He clapped his hands together. "This is wonderful. Not wishing to take anything away from you, Josie, but I myself had thought that the key to everything must reside in Vani. That she knows something that will stagger David and the movie audience. Something that will kill her to bring out."

"Exactly," I agreed. "When Vani does tell him the big secret, she will die. She has to—she won't be able to bear the pain, either emotionally or physically."

My father was excited. "Yes. The secret is devastating for Vani to speak. It is not something she would freely admit under any circumstances. This is all vital. It all fits. Josie, you are brilliant!"

I glowed under his compliments, as any daughter would when her daddy approved. "It's only because I have the best teacher in the whole world," I said.

Right then we were interrupted. Silk had another

hamburger for me. "Don't you want it?" she asked, holding it on a paper plate in front of my face. "You asked for two."

"I cooked it specially for you," Helen called from a nearby table, where she was stuffing herself beside Pascal and Tom. "It's extremely well done."

I had eaten most of my burger. Another bite or two and it would be gone. But a chill suddenly went through me as the wind brushed my bare arms. My fatigue was catching up with me. I would have to go to bed soon and I didn't want my stomach totally jammed.

"I think I'll pass on it," I said.

"But we'll be wasting the food," Silk said. I think that, because she had had a major hand in the creation of the burger, I was personally insulting her.

"Waste not, want not," Helen chipped in, giggling.

"I'll eat it," Tom said.

Silk turned to him. "But you've already had two burgers. You'll make yourself sick."

"If he's hungry, let him eat it," I said, slightly annoyed.

"Tom is still a growing boy," Helen added after a moment.

Silk shrugged and gave the burger to Tom. I set the rest of my meal aside. My stomach wasn't in the best of moods. It must have been all the trauma I had recently gone through, I decided.

"Only one final key," my dad said. "Then we'll have it."

"It'll come," I said.

"It will come through you," he said, admiration in his tone. "When do you think? At the end of the week? The day we leave here? Your muse should visit us one last time, don't you think?"

I nodded. "Yes. But I think she will come sooner than that."

I went inside to bed. I kept my statue of Sryope clasped in my hands as I snuggled under the covers. I knew my dream of Sryope's trial would come. It would be a nightmare. There was no stopping it.

CHAPTER 12

ON THE DAY OF SRYOPE'S TRIAL ALL THE GODS WERE GATH-
ered on Mt. Olympus in the hall of Apollo. There was
much excitement and gossip. Not since Pan had a god
been killed by another god. Most of the gods already
believed that Sryope was guilty of the crime, although
Apollo had sent out a strict order that no one was to
judge until the trial was over. Apollo was to preside
over the trial, but he had decreed that all gods would
vote on Sryope's fate. This pleased the gods who
seldom got to vote on anything important.

Sryope was brought in chains to the center of the
hall. Three days had passed since her capture on Earth
by the Furies, and she had spent the time in a dark
dungeon in Hades. She was frightened, but it glad-
dened her to see Apollo sitting on his throne in front
of her, his robes white, his gold crown bright with the
most precious jewels. She knew that Apollo had the

gift of knowing when truth was spoken and when lies were uttered. She would simply have to say she was innocent and Apollo would defend her. After all, hadn't she worshiped at his feet since she was a child? There was no need to worry, she assured herself and straightened up tall before the assembly.

"Who accuses me?" she spoke defiantly.

"The truth does, Sryope, daughter of Thalia," a powerful voice rang out from one side of the hall. Out walked Minos, clothed in black robes, one of the three gods who judged mortals in the Underworld. The other two, Rhadamanthus and Aeacus, also dressed in black robes, were close at hand. Sryope was confused. Minos was concerned with the judgment of humans. Why was he at her trial? Clearly it was to spearhead the false charges against her. Sryope met his eyes as he approached.

"I did not kill Phthia," Sryope said to Minos. "She was my friend." She turned to Apollo. "Is this not true, O Lord?"

Apollo shrugged. "The assembly will decide what is true and what is false. You must defend yourself, Sryope."

The words stung Sryope, but she knew she was innocent and was confident she could convince the others. "I didn't kill Phthia," she repeated. "I don't even know how she could have been killed. Was she not immortal?"

At this question a stir went through the assembly. Most of the gods, Sryope could see, did not understand how a god could be killed either. Minos stepped in front of her. His eyes, black as his robes, were set like ebony jewels in a face white as polished marble.

"I am going to ask you questions, Sryope," Minos said. "You are to answer them truthfully. If you lie, and we find out you have lied, it will make your punishment that much worse. Do you understand?"

"I am innocent," Sryope responded. "Ask your foolish questions."

Minos was unmoved by her harsh tone. "You have already stated that Phthia was your friend. It is true that you grew up together?"

"Yes," Sryope said.

"You spent many years together?" Minos asked.

"Yes. Everyone knows that."

"During this time, did the two of you ever quarrel?"

"All friends quarrel at one time or another, be they in heaven or on Earth."

"You have not answered the question, Sryope."

"Yes. Phthia and I sometimes quarreled."

"Did you quarrel about Aeneas, who, I understand, is now your husband?"

Sryope hesitated. "It wasn't precisely a quarrel."

"Phthia was with Aeneas before you, was she not?"

"Yes."

"Did he love her?"

"In the beginning, I believe. You should ask him, not me." She could see Aeneas standing in the back of the hall, by the door. His face was distraught. She had not been allowed to speak to him since her capture at the hands of the Furies. The crones were also present, sitting near the front, by themselves. No one could bear to be near them. They emitted the foul stench of dried mortal blood.

"We may ask Aeneas, if it is necessary," Minos said. "But for now we will speak to you alone. Phthia was your friend, as you have stated. Did she love Aeneas?"

"I don't know."

"But being your friend, surely Phthia confided in you. How come you do not know if she loved Aeneas or not?"

"Phthia lusted after many men," Sryope said. "I do not know if she loved any of them, and that includes Aeneas."

"Do you love Aeneas?" Minos asked.

"He is my husband."

"You have not answered the question."

"Yes, I love Aeneas."

"When Phthia was with Aeneas, were you in love with him at that time?"

"I did not know him as well as I know him now. But I was fond of him."

"Were you so fond of him that you thought to take him away from Phthia?"

Sryope knew she had to speak carefully. Minos could call forth many gods to speak against her. She did not know who Phthia had spoken to about Aeneas. Sryope had spoken to no one of her interest in Aeneas until the day she married him. She had learned, on Mt. Olympus, it was best to remain silent about anything important.

"My interest in Aeneas was one of friendship," Sryope said. "That is, until Phthia lost interest in Aeneas and resumed her old habit of pursuing multiple suitors."

"Then you formed a sexual relationship with Aeneas?" Minos asked.

"No. Before Aeneas became involved with Phthia, she made him swear an oath that he would remain faithful to her all the days of his life. I refused to become involved with Aeneas until I felt that oath was no longer binding."

"Did you go to Phthia and ask her to free Aeneas of his oath?"

"No," Sryope said.

"Why not?"

"I believed she would not forgive him the oath."

"So you thought of a plan to force her to revoke the oath?"

"At this time Phthia was with many others. Aeneas wanted to be with me. We were in love. Phthia had not been with Aeneas in a long time."

"You have not answered the question, Sryope."

"It was not a plan but a challenge. This is well known. Who could tell the better tale? Phthia or me? The contest was held here in this hall."

Minos nodded. "I remember. I was present. Tell me, if you won the contest, what were you to gain from Phthia in return?"

"She would forgive Aeneas his oath and we would be free to marry."

"And if Phthia won the contest, what was she to receive from you?"

Sryope stopped to consider. The assembly might have suspected she had secret knowledge that would embarrass Phthia. Because of what happened at the close of the contest, a few must believe the knowledge concerned the identity of Phthia's father. Without her saying, most of the gods would assume she had forced Phthia into the contest. It was probably best she allow a partial truth.

"Phthia was to gain my silence," Sryope said.

"Your silence on what?" Minos asked.

"That I cannot say. I promised Phthia to not speak of it."

"But Phthia is dead. You may speak freely."

"Phthia was my friend. I will not dishonor her by breaking my promise to her. It does not matter to me whether she is with us or not."

Minos moved closer, his bony finger pointed at Sryope's face. "This secret you knew about Phthia—it would have led to her dishonor if others found out?"

Minos was shrewd, Sryope realized. He was trying to trap her with her own words. "Perhaps," she replied.

"But Phthia did not defeat you at the challenge. You are not bound to your end of the bargain."

"I have answered you. She was my friend. I will keep her secret safe in my heart."

At this Minos laughed. "You speak of friendship and your heart. It is clear to all of us that you used this secret to force Phthia into a challenge you knew she could not win."

"I deny that."

Minos moved to score a point. "Then why was Phthia's only reward for winning the contest to be your silence?"

"It was all she asked for." She added, "Phthia had every opportunity to win the contest."

"Now you are being insincere, Sryope. No one on Mt. Olympus—even your mother, Thalia—could defeat you in telling stories. Is that not the truth, Sryope?"

"I have never made such a claim."

"You are too shrewd, Sryope. You let others speak for you so you can appear humble." Minos moved about the hall, making sure he had everyone's attention. "What was the nature of the story you told the day of your challenge with Phthia?"

"You were here. You know the answer to that question."

"I prefer to hear your answer."

"I told a story of a Fury who seduced a goddess and begot a child."

"Did this story have anything to do with Phthia?"

Sryope hesitated. "Not to my knowledge."

"You made the story up?"

"It came to me."

"How did it come to you, Sryope?"

"As all stories do. Out of nothing."

"Do you know who Phthia's father was?"

Again Sryope hesitated. Tyche, Phthia's mother, was also present in the hall. Sryope assumed Phthia had told her mother where she had gained the knowledge of who her father was. Minos could question Tyche and learn this fact. If she lied now, and her lie came out, then she would be condemned for the murder of Phthia, even though she had had nothing to do with it. The gods would simply assume she had lied about everything.

Yet she had already stated that her story had nothing to do with Phthia. She could not go back on her word. She would have to hope that if Tyche was questioned by Minos, she would remain silent as she had done when Phthia had questioned her.

"I don't know who her father was," Sryope said.

"Do you know why Phthia reacted in the contest as if you were telling a story about her?" Minos asked.

"No. Except—"

"Except what?"

"Many times a listener hears a story and sees a part of themselves in the tale, even when the storyteller has no knowledge of the listener."

"Do you think that's what happened to Phthia the day of the contest?" Minos asked.

"I don't know."

"Did you ever see Phthia after that day?"

"No, I did not."

"Did Phthia ever release Aeneas from his oath?"

"Aeneas was to be free of his oath if Phthia lost the contest. This Phthia stated publicly. Phthia ran from the contest—she did not try to compete with me. Therefore, I felt, as did Aeneas, that the oath was no longer binding."

Minos moved close again. "You are fond of mortals, are you not, Sryope?"

"I am."

"Your husband, Aeneas, is half mortal, isn't he?"

"Yes."

"You make frequent trips to Earth, although few gods now visit there. Is that true?"

"Yes."

"Why do you do this? What is there that attracts you?"

"I go to Earth to whisper my tales into the minds of the mortal writers and poets to inspire their work so that they, in turn, may inspire their fellow mortals to lead better lives." Sryope paused. "This was permitted by the great god Zeus himself."

"It was permitted in the past by Zeus," Minos said. "But he is long gone and the ways of men have changed. On Earth it is now the age of science, and mortals have no awareness of spiritual matters. Why, where is the man or woman who still worships us? Answer me."

"It is true that mortals have changed, but they haven't lost all awareness of matters of the spirit, as you say. Their modes of worship have simply changed, like so much else in their lives."

"Are there mortals on Earth anywhere who worship you?"

"No."

"Then why are you so eager to give them your gifts?"

"I have answered this question. I help them so that they may lead better lives."

"Your motives are pure then?" Minos asked.

"If you like."

"Do you do anything else on Earth besides inspire writers and poets?"

"I sometimes go for walks."

"Walks?"

"Yes. In the woods and by the seas. It is a pleasure of mine."

"Do you mettle in the affairs of mortal hearts?"

"Not directly. But my stories can affect the mortal heart."

"In an evil way?"

"It is difficult to say what the effect of every story will be on every mortal. I believe the stories I give to the world are uplifting." Sryope glanced around the assembly. "Haven't I brought inspiration here?"

"I will ask the questions, Sryope," Minos said. "Do you ever turn one mortal against the other?"

"No."

"Have you ever inspired a mortal to hurt another mortal?"

"No. Such an act has been outlawed by Apollo."

"How many mortals do you work with on Earth?"

"Approximately two thousand."

"Do you know them all?"

"Yes."

"Are they all successful in their crafts as a result of your aid?"

"Their success varies. Some are rich and famous. Others are simply happy to share their stories and poems with family and friends. I believe each in his or her own way has benefited from me."

"How do you choose who to help?"

"I am drawn to those who have passion for their work."

Minos stopped in front of Sryope. "You know I am also connected to the affairs of mortals. When their lives are done, my fellow gods, Rhadamanthus and Aeacus, and I judge which path they will take after death."

"I know this is so. But it is also my understanding that not all mortals who die come before you."

Minos was insulted. "Where have you heard this blasphemy spoken?"

"On Mt. Olympus. Many say this. Is it true?"

Minos was angry. "You are not here to challenge my authority. Do you understand, Sryope?"

"You asked the question. I merely answered you."

Minos's anger faded from his face, although Sryope didn't believe it was gone. He took a step backward. "Before a mortal's soul is judged, a review of his or her life is made by us. It is easy for us to see everything a mortal has done. Right now I would like to show you, and the gathered assembly, the image of three different mortals. I want you, Sryope, to tell me if you know them. Do you understand?"

"Yes."

Minos raised his hand. The image of a man appeared in midair in the center of the hall, in colorful detail. The gods leaned forward to see better. Even Apollo stirred. Sryope couldn't understand what Phthia's death had to do with mortals. Surely no one on Earth could have harmed her.

"I know him," Sryope said. "He is a writer. He lives in America."

Minos moved his hand. A young blond woman replaced the image of the man.

"That is the man's daughter," Sryope said.

Minos again tilted his fingers. A young brunette replaced the blond girl.

"That is a friend of the daughter," Sryope said. "I know all three of them."

Minos allowed the last image to fade. "Have you given your stories to the man? Is that how you know him?"

"Yes. Since he was a young man, I have been helping him."

"Have you helped the daughter in any way?" Minos asked.

Sryope considered. "I have helped her, occasionally, with her homework. For example, when she had to write a paper for school, I gave her a touch of inspiration."

"Does this particular girl have a passion for her homework?"

Sryope almost laughed. "No. Few mortal girls do."

"But you said that you are drawn to those who have

passion for their work. Why would you go out of your way to influence this girl?"

"She lives in the same house as the writer I help. While there, I couldn't help but be attracted to her. She is a bright girl and has interests in many things." Sryope shrugged. "I did not influence her as much as I gave her some fresh ideas."

"Could you tell us the nature of the ideas you gave her? That is, if you remember?"

"I have an excellent memory. I can give you one example. I inspired her to write a paper for her class on things mortals could do to help curb the pollution of their oceans and forests."

"Have you ever inspired her to hurt someone?"

Sryope felt a flush of anger. "That is an absurd question. And you have already asked it and I have already answered it. I help mortals, I do not hurt them."

"That remains to be seen, Sryope. The third image, the picture of the friend—have you ever influenced her?"

"No."

"How do you know her then?"

"Since the girls were young, they have occasionally spent nights at each others' houses. I observed the young brunette girl at the writer's house and I recognize her from there."

"Would you say, from what you have observed, that the girls are friends?"

"Yes."

"You are sure of this?" Minos asked.

"Yes."

"What would you say if I told you the daughter of the writer had tried to kill the other girl?"

Sryope was shocked. "I would have trouble believing it."

"Why?"

"I have already answered that question. They are friends. Why would one try to kill the other?"

Minos leaned close and once more pointed a bony finger at her. His eyes were as cold as black stones on a winter night.

"That is what we are trying to find out, Sryope. When we have the answer to this question, we will have the answer to how Phthia was killed, and why she was killed, and who killed her."

"I did not kill Phthia," Sryope repeated for the third time.

Minos grinned. He had no teeth. "You did worse than kill her."

CHAPTER 13

I AWOKE TO A DULL ACHE IN MY ABDOMEN. EARLY MORNING light shone through the windows. Helen slept silently on her bed. I got up and went to the bathroom, then returned to bed. But I couldn't go back to sleep because the ache remained. I assumed I had gas from Silk's special sauce. I decided to go for a walk along the water. After dressing quickly, I slipped out of our room without disturbing Helen.

The morning was chillier than previous ones. There were high clouds, and even though the sun was up it couldn't be seen. I headed down the beach, away from town. The foam of spent waves rushed over my sandals. I didn't enjoy my walk. The pains in my stomach wouldn't go away. I began to wonder if it really was gas pains.

Half an hour later found me back at the hotel,

sitting in the lounge and drinking coffee I didn't want. I felt lousy and tired. My attention was evenly divided between my aching body and my dream of Sryope's trial. I didn't know if I was disappointed or relieved that I had awakened before the verdict was delivered. The memory of Minos and his questions made me shiver. And those foul-smelling Furies sitting up front and giggling over Sryope's discomfort—what a disgustingly ugly bunch of bitches. But I would have liked to have the whole dream business over with and settled. I knew I had one nightmare left to dream.

I decided to call Tom. He'd told me he was an early riser. I'd memorized his number when he'd given it to me. I have an excellent memory for details.

Pascal answered the phone. I knew the two of them lived together. "Pascal," I said, "this is Josie. Is Tom up?"

"Yes, Tom is awake, but he is—ill."

"What?"

"Sick." Pascal's voice was anxious. "I am thinking to take him to health center in town, but I don't know. He says he will feel better soon."

"Can I talk to him?"

"He is in toilet now."

"What are his symptoms?" I asked.

"Excuse, please?"

"Ah, never mind. Can you give me directions to your place? I think I should come over."

"Please come."

It took me some time to understand the directions,

but eventually I felt that I could find their apartment without getting lost. I returned to my room for the keys to my motor scooter. Helen continued enjoying the repose of Pan, I thought, and didn't ask myself how I knew Pan had been a deep sleeper. Picking up my keys, I realized I was leaving without taking my statue of Sryope. I found it under the blankets where I had left it. With the pain in my gut, I hadn't even bothered to look at it when I had gone out earlier.

I almost dropped the statue when I picked it up. I was lucky I didn't let out a cry. The marble material was now almost entirely gone from the goddess. She now appeared to be made out of a clear crystal of some kind. I studied it more closely. The crystal appeared to encase a colorless liquid. The statue was hollow.

I stuffed Sryope into one of my jeans pockets.

I'd show her to Tom, I thought.

But I still wasn't going to let him touch her.

I left a note on the chest of drawers explaining that I had gone to Tom's and that he wasn't feeling well. I left Tom's phone number for Helen.

It was approximately eight o'clock when I climbed onto my motor scooter. I had my windbreaker on; my camera was in the side pocket, where I had zipped it during my first visit to Delos. Like I really needed the thing. Tom wasn't going to want me to take his picture while he was feeling sick. I transferred Sryope to the opposite pocket in my windbreaker. I thought she'd be safer there.

On the ride over to the guys' apartment I felt really sick. My pain had moved. I was feeling more discomfort in my back than in my abdomen. I tried taking long, slow, deep breaths, but they had no effect at all on it. I wondered if Tom and I had caught some kind of flu bug. We had kissed enough to have the same germs.

Tom and Pascal's place was a tiny apartment located above a clothes shop at the other end of town. I parked my scooter in the back as Pascal had advised and took the rickety wooden steps up to the second floor. Pascal was at the door before I finished knocking. My anxiety leapfrogged when I saw how anxious he was.

"Tom is ill," Pascal said quickly.

He showed me in. The apartment was tidy and lined with books. There was a small living room attached to an even tinier kitchen. Two box-like bedrooms squared off a two-step hallway in the back. Tom's bedroom door was open. He was turning over in bed as I entered. He had his underwear on, nothing else. There was a gray pallor to his skin. He tried to smile for my benefit but it was strained.

"Hi, Josie," he muttered. "How do you like our place?"

I sat on the bed beside him and took his hand. He was soaked with sweat, although I couldn't detect a fever. "Your place is wonderful. What are your symptoms?"

He grimaced. "I ache all over."

"Does your throat hurt?"

"Yes. My head, my back. My legs and arms even hurt. I've never felt like this." He struggled to take a breath. "It started during the night."

"You have to go to the doctor."

"I don't want to go to the doctor. I hate them."

"It doesn't matter what you want," I said firmly. "You could have meningitis or something weird like that for all we know. You're going and that's settled. Don't even bother to argue with me." I glanced at Pascal, who stood worrying in the doorway. "Do you have your truck?"

He nodded vigorously. *"Le camion* parked in the street."

"Go get it. Park it at the end of the stairway. Keep the engine running. We'll be down in two minutes."

"In two minutes," Pascal repeated as he left.

"What kind of hospital do they have on this island?" I asked Tom as I searched for a pair of pants in the closet.

"They call it the health center. It's small and the doctor on duty usually doesn't speak English."

"I don't believe you. This is a tourist island. Any doctor here should speak English."

He smiled again briefly. "You should be a nurse when you grow up, Josie. You have the knack. You—" His face suddenly contorted in pain and he doubled up. "Oh, God," he whispered.

I jumped to his side and wiped the sweat that poured from his forehead. "What is it?" I asked. A stupid question.

"Pain, incredible pain," he gasped. "It's like there's something inside me trying to kill me."

I continued to stroke him and spoke gently. "I won't let it kill you, Tom. Remember, I owe you for saving my life. It will have to kill me first to get to you."

I didn't feel as bad as he did, but I did not feel so hot myself. Now was not the time to talk about myself, but I did wonder if we had the same thing. Of course, I also wondered what it was.

That it should strike so swiftly.

The Mykonos health center was tiny, but the two doctors impressed me as extremely competent. One was old, the other middle-aged. They took Tom in immediately. If anything, his pain was getting worse, but he was aware enough to describe his condition. Pascal and I sat down in the reception area to wait. Not long after that the old doctor came out and said they'd have to run a few tests. It looked as if it would be a long wait. I asked the man if he had any idea what the problem was and he just shook his head.

"This is not the way I had this day planned," I told Pascal.

Pascal kept shifting uneasily in his seat. His nerves were wound tight. "Not a good day," he agreed.

I had begun to perspire heavily. The pain in my back had moved into my neck and shoulders, although it hadn't actually left my spine. This wasn't a good sign. Still, I wanted to leave the doctors to concentrate on Tom. My decision wasn't entirely noble. I hated doctors poking at me.

"Tom said you two met here," I said. "Was it really in a bar?"

Pascal shook his head. "We meet in town. There is bad man there—takes *legumes* and say I cheat him. But I no cheat anyone. I tell him that and he shove me to ground. I get mad, I don't like to be shoved. I am no . . . afraid. I hit him but he pull out knife." Pascal measured a foot and a half with his hands and shook his head again. "Big knife. He go to stick me with it. But Tom suddenly there. He kick knife from man's hand. Then I hit man in the face and he fall to the ground." Pascal smiled at the memory. "His face all bloody."

I remembered on the beach how smoothly Tom had kicked the book from my hands. I wondered if he had taken martial arts training, and made a mental note to ask him.

"How long ago was that?" I asked, putting a hand to my head. The pain was not stopping. There was suddenly pressure behind my eyeballs that was record setting. It was as if I had a tiny alien in the center of my brain that wanted to hatch.

"Two years," Pascal said.

I coughed. "And you've been friends since?"

"Yes. Tom is good friend."

I smiled. "I know. He's a great guy."

Pascal looked at me strangely. "Are you sick?"

He had enough to worry about. "No. I'm just—tired."

"You sweat."

A wave of dizziness swept over me. I had to brace

my arm on my knee to steady myself. "That's just something American girls do when we get hot," I mumbled.

"Josie?"

I bent over but managed to give him a smile. "Yes, Pascal?"

"You are not well."

I nodded. "I feel a bit off. Maybe I will just go to the bathroom and then I'll feel better. OK?"

"Let me help you," he said, taking my arm. I brushed him aside.

"In America girls go to the bathroom by themselves." I stood up, with great effort. "You just stay here. I'll be back in a minute. I'll be fine—don't worry about me, Pascal. OK?"

He was scared. "OK," he said.

It made me chuckle to hear him say that word.

I started for the restroom.

A pain, as thick as the trunk of a tree and as bright as lightning, shot through my body from my feet to my head. My vision exploded in red. Then everything went black and I felt myself falling. Yet it seemed I never hit the floor but simply bypassed it on my long descent into the Underworld, where Minos and the others waited to judge the souls of mortals.

CHAPTER 14

"HAVE YOU EVER DREAMED OF BECOMING A MORTAL?"
Minos asked Sryope.

"No," Sryope said. "Why should I have such a dream? It is not possible for an immortal to become mortal."

"But if it were possible, would it be something you'd desire?"

"Is this another of your foolish questions?"

"You will answer it, Sryope, lest we all assume you are afraid to answer it."

Sryope spoke proudly. "I am afraid of nothing. No, I would not choose to be one if it were possible."

"Why not?" Minos asked.

"Because mortals are mortal. They grow old and die. Their lives are beset with calamities. They suffer illness, wounds to their bodies, the limits of being

163

confined to the surface of the Earth. These are not things any god or goddess would desire."

Minos nodded. "Your answer is reasonable. This court will now move to the heart of the accusations against you."

"Thank Zeus for that," Sryope mumbled.

Minos spoke bitterly. "You are proud, Sryope. You spend your gifts freely over the surface of the Earth, where your fellow gods have counseled you not to walk, and then you dole out what favors strike your mood on Mt. Olympus."

"You are not from Mt. Olympus and know not what I do here," Sryope said. "You know only the dead."

Minos nodded. "I know the dead. Unlike the gods, I have a record of each day, each minute of a mortal's life. I have the record of that writer you say you inspire, and his daughter, and the friend of the daughter. I can show these records to this assembly."

Sryope was undaunted. She understood what Minos was doing. He did not, could not, have a record of a god, who never died, and who would never stand before him in the Underworld for judgment. But Minos could follow her actions where she had interacted with mortals. There she would be revealed on his moving images.

"Go ahead," Sryope said. "My relationship with them is above reproach."

Minos spoke to the whole assembly. "We will now see images from the times Sryope troubled the lives of these three mortals."

The pictures appeared in midair in the center of the

164

hall like holograms. Sryope nodded to herself as they swiftly swept from one scene to the next. Most of the images showed her sitting still beside the father as he worked at his desk, whispering ideas and words into his mortal mind. On occasion, though, she was shown touching the daughter, the blond girl, on the head. At these touches, the girl would always smile. Never was there an image of Sryope with the friend of the daughter.

Minos stopped the moving images for a moment.

"Are these scenes accurate, Sryope?" he asked.

"Yes."

"You were there in the mortals' house? That was you we saw?"

"Yes."

"While you were in their house, did you ever once see another god?"

"No."

"You are sure of that?"

"You have a habit, Minos, of asking the same question again and again."

He did not like her. "And you have a habit of answering these same questions differently each time. Answer this one."

"I am sure I was never in the house of these mortals when another god was present. I would have known if another had come."

"We will continue." Minos held up his hand. The images resumed.

At first Sryope noticed nothing unusual with the records. There were more pictures of her helping the father and the daughter. Then came one scene where the daughter had the brown-haired friend over for the night. As they settled down to rest, in the blond girl's bedroom, Sryope was not present. But when the light was turned off, a goddess suddenly entered the room through the ceiling. Sryope peered closely. It was her, she could see it was herself.

But Sryope didn't remember entering the bedroom that night.

On the record, Sryope did not stay in the room long. But she did pause long enough to touch the forehead of each of the sleeping girls. The girls grimaced with the touch and stirred uneasily. Then Sryope left.

Minos halted the images.

"Was that you in the bedroom?" he asked.

Sryope was confused. It was true she had a fine memory, but occasionally things happened that she had trouble recalling. Yet she was almost sure she had never touched the girl with the brown hair.

"I don't know," Sryope said.

"You don't know?" Minos asked. "It certainly looked like you. It must have been you."

"Yes, I suppose," Sryope said. "But—"

"Yes?"

"I have no recollection of having touched the friend's forehead."

"But we have just seen you touch her, Sryope," Minos said. "What inspiration did you pour into her sleeping mind?"

"I have already stated that I don't remember having done anything to her."

"Earlier you stated that you had definitely never influenced the friend. Is that not true?"

Sryope shrugged. "It's possible I made an error."

"It's very possible you made a grave error," Minos said. He raised his hand. The images continued.

This scene was almost identical to the last one. The friend of the daughter had come over to spend the night. They talked together for some time and then turned off the light. When the girls were asleep Sryope saw herself again enter the bedroom through the ceiling. This detail struck Sryope as peculiar. Ordinarily she entered a mortal house through the window. Once more she had no memory of what was being shown.

The Sryope in the hologram put her hand on the forehead of the daughter, who shook violently in bed at the touch and let out a soft moan. Before she awakened the goddess moved on to the friend and touched her on the head. The friend also cringed under the immortal fingers. But the goddess soon let go and stood staring down at them both. Several minutes went by.

Then the friend climbed out of the bed and walked to the window. She raised the window. The bedroom was on the second story of the house. The friend began to climb out the window. The goddess smiled. The daughter, still in bed, awoke with a start and let out a cry.

The daughter saved the friend from climbing out the window. The friend seemed to awaken as if from a trance and acted embarrassed. The goddess vanished, and the girls went back to sleep.

Minos stopped the images.

"Was that you in the room that night, Sryope?" he asked.

"No." Now she was certain. She would have remembered such a night.

"We just saw that it was you."

"It was not me. I am certain. I never influenced the friend of the daughter to try to climb out the window."

"Then who was it in that room with those girls?"

"I don't know. Someone who looks like me."

Minos was amused. "Is there anyone in this assembly who resembles you that closely?"

"No. But—"

"Yes? Speak your mind, Sryope. You have never hesitated to speak it before."

"I don't know where these images have come from."

Minos was angry. "You challenge me? These are the records that are used to judge a mortal's soul at the end of his life. Even Apollo himself would not dispute them." Minos turned to Apollo. "Is that not so, my Lord?"

Apollo nodded. "The records are not to be questioned."

Sryope drew in a deep breath and trembled. Her confusion deepened. Apollo could not be lying, yet she had not done these things.

"Do you have anything to say?" Minos asked.

Sryope drew herself up once more. She must not appear frightened, she knew, or the assembled gods would be sure of her guilt. "Yes. I insist that there was an impostor in the room that night with those girls, someone posing as me."

Minos laughed long, his voice like the cackle of a jackal. When he was done, he said, "Who is this impostor, Sryope?"

"I don't know."

"Who do you know who has the power to appear as you?"

"I don't know."

"If you do not know these things, then how can you say that there is such an impostor?"

"Because I know I would never have done anything to hurt those girls," Sryope said.

"Because you are not a hateful being? Is that what you are saying?"

"Yes."

"Phthia, if she was here, might disagree." Minos turned to speak to the assembly. "These records are indisputable. There is no impostor. What we are seeing is the truth." He paused and raised his hand. "Now we will see the last two records, what happened five and four days before Phthia's body was found floating lifeless in the River Styx."

The images sprang to life. The scene had shifted. Sryope did not recognize it at first, but as it unfolded she came to understand that they were now in the bedroom of the friend. This time the daughter of the writer was sleeping over at the friend's house.

The friend had a smaller house; the bedroom was tiny. The friend offered the daughter her bed and the daughter accepted it, while the friend spread blankets on the floor for herself. They spoke for a while, then turned off the light and slept.

Sryope entered the room through the ceiling again.

"No," Sryope whispered. She had never been to the friend's house.

The goddess went first to the daughter of the writer. This time she put one hand on the girl's forehead and the other over the girl's heart. The goddess closed her eyes and the girl began to writhe on the bed. Then the goddess released her and stood watching for several minutes. The blond girl settled back down. It seemed she had gone back to sleep. But then suddenly she sat up in bed. Her eyes were open but empty as a night sky filled with clouds of smoke.

The blond girl climbed out of bed and went into her friend's bathroom, which adjoined the bedroom. Leaving the light off, she removed a bottle of pills from the medicine cabinet and began to pull open the capsules. One by one, she emptied the powder in the pills into a glass of water. She did this until all the pills were gone.

Then the girl picked up the glass and began to carry it toward her friend, who slept on the floor. The goddess watched all this with a smile on her face.

But the blond girl suddenly stopped and the vacant expression in her eyes was replaced by awareness. As she took in the poisoned glass of water in her hand, her arm shook. She started back toward the bathroom.

The goddess was on her in a moment.

The girl, no longer asleep now, was difficult to lead. The goddess had to use ten times the power to influence her to give the poison to her friend, who continued to rest undisturbed on the floor. The goddess thrust both her hands deep into the blond girl's chest and the girl weakened under the attack, sagging against the wall, the glass of poisoned water still in her hand. The girl let out a cry and began to choke as if she were having a heart attack. But she held on to the glass because the goddess wouldn't let her drop it. Slowly, steadily, she stood back up and walked toward her friend, who had finally begun to stir.

The goddess didn't let go of the blond girl's heart. Sryope saw she had no intention of releasing her until the girl had given the drink to her friend, until she was fully implicated in the crime that was taking place. But Sryope watched with a measure of pride as the blond girl once more began to resist the evil power of the impostor. Even as the goddess gripped the mortal's heart as tightly as she could, and whispered spells woven with obscene words, the blond girl was able to turn away from her friend and set the glass on a bookshelf.

When the blond girl let go of the glass, the goddess became incensed and released her. The girl was panting hard and clutching her chest. She looked around the room as if seeing it anew and not liking how it had changed. Then she fled the room in her pajamas. The record did not show the daughter of the writer leaving the house, but the sound of a slamming door was heard.

The goddess swore bitterly and turned her attention to the friend, who had sat up on the floor awake with the sound of the slamming door. The goddess did not give the girl a chance to catch her wits. She plunged her hands into the girl's heart and the girl let out a whimper and turned toward the glass of poisoned water resting on the bookshelf above her. The goddess dragged the girl to her feet. The goddess made the girl pick up the glass. Then the goddess—she must have been a demon, Sryope thought—made the girl drink the poison down to the last drop.

The goddess released the mortal. It was not long before the girl collapsed on the floor. The goddess left.

Minos halted the images.

"Did you do these things to these girls, Sryope?" he asked.

Sryope shook her head. "Never."

"Who did?"

"I don't know."

"Your claims of innocence sound weaker and weaker."

"I didn't do any of these horrible things!"

"You did worse things!" Minos yelled. He raised his hand.

Another scene of evil unfolded for the gods to judge her by.

The friend, the girl with the brown hair, lay in a

hospital bed. She was obviously very ill. Tubes led into her body. Wires were attached to her head and heart, and monitors that traced green lines and emitted annoying beeping sounds stood on both sides of her bed. The girl had a plastic mask over her mouth and nose. She was hardly breathing.

The impostor Sryope plunged through the ceiling. She had Phthia with her.

"No!" Sryope cried in the midst of the assembly.

The pictures didn't stop. The goddess had Phthia's neck in a thorny noose. Phthia struggled, terrified, with the noose, but could not break free. The goddess appeared all powerful. Dragging Phthia with her, she strode to the dying girl and spat on the mortal's chest. The saliva came out blood-red.

The monitor beside the bed began to emit a high-pitched beep.

"Alecto," Sryope whispered to herself.

The girl's heart had stopped.

Doctors rushed into the hospital room and began to work on her.

The Fury. The impostor was Phthia's father, Sryope realized, the one who had impregnated Tyche. Who could say what was the sex of a demon? Sryope realized she should have seen the truth earlier. There was only one class of beings that could change shape and fool a god—the Furies. Had that not been the way Tyche had been seduced in the first place? Also, the thorny noose around Phthia's neck was the same one Alecto had used to bind Sryope when she had been captured on Earth.

The doctors applied pads to the girl's chest.

Electrical shocks were sent into the girl's heart.

The body leapt off the bed.

The heart did not start.

The doctors tried again.

The monitors had gone silent.

The doctors began to back away. One man said she was gone.

The goddess, the Fury Alecto, grabbed the screaming Phthia by the hair and let out a wicked laugh. She thrust Phthia into the girl's body.

The monitors in the hospital room began to beep again.

The doctors reacted with joy. They began to work on the girl again.

The Fury pulled back on Phthia's suddenly limp body.

The girl on the bed opened her eyes.

Alecto fled the hospital room with Phthia's lifeless goddess body in her noose. They descended through the floor this time. But no one in the assembly could see that it was a Fury.

Because it looked exactly like Sryope. Just like her.

Sryope understood.

Alecto had forced Phthia's soul into the body of the girl the moment the mortal's soul had fled. There was after all, Sryope realized, a way for an immortal to become a mortal.

The records of Minos came to an end.

The silence in the hall was deep.

Minos stepped up to Sryope. "Do you have anything to say?" he asked.

Sryope glanced at the crone, Alecto. The Fury was smiling, its hideous dog's head dripping human blood on the floor at its feet. The demon understood that Sryope had divined the evil scheme, but the crone also understood that no one would believe Sryope if she tried to prove her innocence. She could not go back and deny her earlier statements, while trying to explain how the Fury was capable of changing form. She could not admit to knowing who Phthia's father was. Minos had built up the case against her from many angles. The records were merely the last stroke.

Sryope wondered if Alecto had fooled even Minos, if he was not merely a puppet in this vast play. She supposed she would never know.

Sryope appealed to Apollo. "You know, O Lord, that I am innocent," she said. "Can you not save me, your humble servant?"

Apollo was unmoved. "It is your responsibility, Sryope, to save yourself."

Sryope lowered her head. "Then there is nothing I can say." She turned to Minos. "I will await your decision on my punishment."

Minos nodded solemnly. "All the gods will decide what is a fit punishment for you, Sryope. If there is a punishment great enough."

Sryope was thrown into a prison cell on Mt. Olympus while the gods conferred. There were no guards and none was needed. The prison walls were stone taken from the center of the Earth, and the iron bars had been wrought by Hephaestus himself, the famed but ugly god of blacksmiths. There was no possibility of escape. Sryope was alone with her thoughts.

"Apollo leaves me to this unrighteous punishment," she said aloud to herself. "Although he knows I am innocent. Why?"

She could not understand his mind. But even though he had abandoned her in her hour of need, Sryope found it impossible to resent Apollo. Indeed, as she waited for her punishment, which she knew would be horrible, she prayed to him.

"O Lord," she said. "I did commit wrong by forcing Phthia to a challenge I knew she could not win. And I did wish to break her pride when I told the disguised story of her true parentage. I see now it is my own pride that has been shattered. So be it. But I did these things out of love for Aeneas and had no real desire to harm Phthia. I ask for your forgiveness, Apollo, at this time of my doom. I only pray you can hear me, and that your grace will be with me no matter what happens."

Minos came for Sryope not long after. He stood outside the iron bars and read aloud her sentence from a scroll of gold paper, while she sat on the floor of the prison cell.

"It has been decreed by the gods of Olympus and the deities of the Underworld that you, Sryope, daughter of Thalia, should suffer the same fate as Phthia. You are to be taken this moment by Alecto, chief of the Furies, to Earth. There your soul is to be thrust into the body of the daughter of the writer whose heart now burns with disease as a result of the

touch of your filthy hands, and who this very moment
lies near death in a mortal hospital. Your divinity is to
be stripped from you, Sryope, and you are to wander a
helpless mortal among mortals, until the day your
body falls and your soul is brought before me in the
Underworld, where, I assure you, you will be judged
most harshly." Minos paused. "Have you any last
words, Sryope?"

"Yes." She stood up and smoothed her robe. "First,
I would say once more that I am innocent of these
crimes. Second, I am not surprised Alecto has volun-
teered to inflict my punishment, since the crone is the
true perpetrator of all these crimes. Finally, my divinity cannot be stripped from me. I am a child of the
immortal light—it is what I am. Whether I am in
heaven or Earth, or even in the dungeons of hell, I will
always be Sryope."

"Proud words," Minos acknowledged with a slight
bow.

She held his eye. "You will not see me again, Minos.
I have the gift of prophecy. I know it."

Minos did not speak. He turned to the side. Alecto
was suddenly there, her thorny noose in hand, blood,
as always, dripping from the side of her canine mouth.
The prison door was thrust open, the noose was
thrown around Sryope's neck. Alecto grinned fiend-
ishly and Sryope felt a hard yank. She was being
pulled through the floor, through region upon region
of light, until finally the light faded and she was in the
hospital room of the daughter of the writer. It was
true, the girl was dying. The doctors were gathered

around her bed. The beeps on the monitors had ceased. Alecto bent her head toward the lifeless body.

"I will remember this," Sryope told Alecto. "I will avenge myself."

"You will remember," the crone agreed. "But the memory will come to you too late. Phthia will always be one step ahead of you. Your mortal life will be short and end in bitterness. Then you will be with me in hell for eternity."

"Apollo," Sryope started to pray. But at that moment she was thrust into the body of the dead girl.

And the girl opened her eyes and looked around.

The doctors were relieved.

CHAPTER 15

I OPENED MY EYES AND LOOKED AROUND. I WAS IN A HOSPI-
tal bed in a small white room that smelled of rubbing
alcohol. The two doctors at the Mykonos health center
were present, as were my father, Silk, and Helen. My
friend sat on the side of the bed near me and held my
hand. The doctors appeared worried. I was in excruci-
ating pain—my entire body felt as if it were about to
explode.

"How do you feel, Jo?" my father asked. The poor
man. The previous night I had drowned on him and
tonight I was in the grip of a deadly disease. I could
see it was late from the dark window above me. I must
have been unconscious the entire day. I forced a smile
for my father's benefit.

"I hope it's not morning sickness," I said.

My father nodded, his eyes moist. "Wouldn't that

be a tragedy of epic proportions?" He paused. "Are you in pain?"

I nodded weakly. "My whole body."

The doctors conferred. I heard them say the words "The same as the boy." My father sat on the bed beside Helen, who continued to hold my hand. I would have preferred holding my father's.

"The doctors don't know what is wrong with you yet," my dad said. "But they've decided, and I agree with them, that you and Tom—"

"How is Tom?" I asked. Sweat poured from my forehead into my eyes. The pain was so intense it was difficult to talk. My throat was bone-dry. Helen picked up a tissue and dabbed at my skin.

"He is resting right now," my dad said. "The doctors just gave him a shot of morphine. They can give you one if you like. In half an hour there will be a plane ready to fly you both to Athens. They have better facilities there. They will find out what the problem is."

"Sounds like a plan," I mumbled. I was surprised to see that Silk had been crying as well. The kindly elderly doctor also appeared anxious. Only Helen was keeping her cool.

"Would you like something for the pain?" my dad asked.

I took a breath. "Soon. I'd like to talk to Helen alone for a few minutes first. Oh, where is Tom?"

My father stood up and nodded to a closed door on the side wall. "He's resting next door." He squeezed my hand. "You'll be on the plane together, and I'll be there as well. Who knows, Jo, if you're feeling up to it maybe you can help me finish the story."

"We will finish it, Dad," I promised him. "Love you."

"Love you," he said.

Silk stepped forward and leaned over to give me a hug. "You get better, Josie, you hear? I need you to sober up my life. You're the only one who can help me."

"You'll be fine," I said, and there was a note of goodbye in my voice. Silk heard it, I believe—her eyes filled once more.

They left me alone with Helen, who watched me intently.

"Could I have a glass of water, please?" I asked.

She let go of my hand and got me one from a corner sink. She held the water to my lips as I sipped. It tasted like vinegar and I coughed. "Not too much," Helen cautioned.

I nodded for her to take away the glass and then lay back on the pillow. There wasn't much light in the room, just a single tired lamp in the corner. There were shadows everywhere, especially on Helen's face.

It was not as hard as one might imagine for me to accept the truth. I think the thing is, I had always known, since I had left the hospital after my heart trouble, that I was different from other people. I just hadn't known how different.

"I guess the cosmic secret is out of the bag," I said.

Helen nodded gravely. "I took it out of the bag a year ago."

"You were holding my hand when I was unconscious just now. Was that to watch my dream with me?"

"Yes. It was quite a trial, Josie. Or should I call you Sryope? I wish I had been there the first time around."

I wished I had the glass in my hand. I could have thrown the water in her face. "You are a goddamn bitch," I whispered. "What did you do, poison the two of us?"

"Ground-up glass," Helen said. "Fine as dust. I mixed it in with the hamburger when Silk wasn't looking. You put so much garbage on your burgers, I knew you wouldn't notice. You ordered two, so I put the glass in the two. But Tom ended up with the other." She shrugged. "He never treated me right anyway."

"What does ground-up glass do to the insides of a mortal?"

Helen's eyes shone. "You're suffering from a million micro hemorrhages. Your insides are bleeding. There is nothing that can be done to save either of you. Once the glass has been absorbed by the system, it stays in the system." She nodded. "You will die in horrible pain."

"Well, that's lovely, witch."

Helen's face darkened. "My name is Phthia. I'm a goddess."

"You're a witch from hell and you know it."

"It is you who will be going to hell soon, not I. You know, Josie, I have friends in high places."

I shifted weakly in the bed, pain radiating from every nerve in my body. "You have a father in the lowest place. You only feigned fear when you were thrust in that body. You knew the records would be reviewed by Minos. Tell me, was he in on your scheme?"

"No. But he played the role we wanted him to play."

I shook my head in disgust. "So you ran to Daddy when I embarrassed you in front of the others. You never could handle your own problems. But I have to admit, you went to great lengths to get back at me."

"Thank you."

"I'm not complimenting you. I think you are a fool. You had to fall as far as me to get me in this predicament."

"I don't know, Josie, I like being mortal."

"You will die just like me. In a few years that body will be dust."

Helen nodded. "Then I will obtain a fresh one. My father will help me. It is not so hard for a Fury to get what it wants."

"What will your *father* want in return?"

"What every Fury wants—human flesh." Helen stared into the distance. "Tonight I will make a sacrifice to my benefactor on top of Kynthos."

"Delos is sacred. The gods of Olympus have never sanctioned human sacrifices."

Helen chuckled. "The Furies sanctioned them before the gods of Olympus were born. And it will please them doubly that the sacrifice should happen in a place that defiles Apollo."

I regretted I was too weak to strike at her. "Tom is soon going to Athens with me. You will not have him."

"Oh, I'm not talking about Tom. I will use Pascal. I have already talked him into taking me to Delos tonight. He's at the dock now, getting his boss's boat ready."

"But you like Pascal."

"This mortal body pretends to like him. This goddess will use him as she sees fit."

I was appalled. Her behavior, for the entire past year, had been an act. I thought of Zeus's warning to Tyche, so long ago. The witch will be that harder to see. . . .

"Pascal will not leave Tom to take you to the island," I said.

Helen was proud. "He will do whatever I wish. You are not the only one with power, Josie. Even on Olympus, you never suspected how powerful I was."

I snorted. "Your ego was powerful, nothing else. I know why you wanted to get me on Earth with you. You knew in heaven you could not compete with me. I know why you decided to kill me now. Because I had beaten you once more. I had stolen a young man's love from you. Face it, you just couldn't turn Tom on. Admit it, Helen—or Phthia, or whatever you're to be called. You have an inferiority complex."

Helen was bitter. "Your mouth is all you ever had over me. It is all you have now. You and your silly stories—of what use are they to you now? You are in pain, and your pain is only going to increase. Then you will die and Alecto will be waiting for you with the thorny noose."

"I am not afraid of Alecto."

Helen stood up from the bed. "You should be. I spent years with the crone after you tried to humiliate me. I know what goes on down there. It is not something that can be spoken about with mortal words."

"Are you leaving now? Is this goodbye after such a wonderful year together? I don't get you, Helen. Why did you even bother to take me to Delos when you were just going to kill me when you felt like it? You knew the island would trigger my memories."

"Because I wanted Sryope to know who had defeated her."

I laughed. "You wanted Sryope to beg Phthia for mercy. Well, do I look ready to beg, witch? Do I look defeated? Do I look scared?"

Helen was grave. "You will be scared when the end comes. Ralph was."

"What did you do to Ralph?"

"Introduced him to my father. Poor Ralph—died of very unnatural causes." She turned for the door. "Goodbye, Sryope."

"It ain't over until the fat Fury sings!" I called after her as she slammed the door shut.

It is hard, in many ways, to be a mortal once you've realized you used to be a goddess. What I wanted to do was leap out of bed, fly through the air, and rain

185

down a few thunderbolts on Helen. The worst thing about being human was the pain the body could feel. As I sat up in the bed, I felt as if every blood vessel in my system was quietly being scratched open.

I was determined not to feel sorry for myself. I had promised Alecto that I would avenge myself, and I had every intention of doing so. But I needed Tom's help—or, rather, I believed that if I could get him to Delos, on top of Kythnos, the seat of Apollo's power on Earth, I might be able to help him. It was a fact the doctors weren't going to be able to do anything for him except keep him sedated until the end came. Yet my desire to get Tom to Delos was simply based on a feeling I had—that it was the right thing to do. Even as a goddess I had not had the gift of healing. But my feelings were significant; I possessed, after all, the intuition of a muse.

Before rising from the bed I reached over and picked up a pen and piece of paper that were on the bedstand. I had promised my father we would finish the story and we would. Knowing I was wasting precious time, I still wrote him a long note. I intended to leave it for him on my pillow.

Dad,

I know how the story is supposed to end. The alien home world is really the Earth. Yes, I know the aliens destroyed it, and that is true—but only in a certain sense. There are no aliens in this story. The people now on Earth are human beings—or were once human. But they have ruined their planet with pollution and wars and radiation. Over the centuries, they have mutated until they look alien. For that reason their ancestors, the people who first left for the stars, hate them. It's like children who become ashamed of what their parents are. In this story it is the good guys who are the bad guys. The humans want the Earth destroyed so they won't have the embarrassment of their mutated parentage hanging over their heads as they spread across the galaxy. At the same time, Vani and her people are not above blame. They did ruin the Earth, and for that they are sorry. Vani will tell this truth to your hero, David Herrick, just before she dies.

I have a secret to tell you, Dad. I'm not a human or an alien. I'm an angel, your muse, and you won't be seeing me in the days to come. I'm sorry, I know it will be painful for you. But I'll be fine—I have to return to heaven. I know you won't understand a word of this, but if you ever need inspiration in the future, then just close your eyes and think of me and I will be there. Then maybe you will understand a tiny bit. I will be watching from the sky when you receive the Academy Award for your screenplay.

I love you, I have loved you longer than you know.

Your Josie

CHAPTER 16

MY CLOTHES WERE LYING ON A CHAIR IN THE CORNER BESIDE the tired lamp. I was grateful to see no one had disturbed my statue of—myself. The marble artifact had undergone a complete transformation now. It was now totally crystalline, and the liquid inside had turned red. Indeed, it looked like blood. Was it symbolic of my own internal bleeding?

I believed there was meaning in the statue. I knew it was a gift from one of the gods to me, although I didn't know who had set it beside me on Delos. In a sense, for a goddess to be transformed into a mortal ran parallel to a mortal being transformed into stone. The god who had left it may have done so as a personal acknowledgment that I had been unfairly condemned to the Earth. Yet now the stone had changed to crystal. Did that mean I was ready to return to Mt. Olympus? I had serious doubts about that, no matter what I had written in my letter to my father, and no matter how defiantly I had spoken to Helen before she left.

I *was* scared of meeting Alecto.

I dressed and hurriedly entered Tom's room, using the side door. Moving made my pain twice as bad. He was sitting up in bed in his clothes. I assumed he had put his clothes on, or someone had helped him into them, in anticipation of our flight to Athens. He did not appear to be in great pain, but there was a film over his eyes. I attributed the latter to the morphine they had given him.

"Josie," he said softly. "I hear you have the same thing I've got, you poor dear."

I sat on the bed beside him. The sweat was pouring off me in quarts. "Tom, my darling, we don't have a virus. We have been poisoned."

He lifted an inquiring eyebrow. He was a bit slow, but still sharp enough. I assumed the shot, though, would wear off before we could reach Delos.

"Who poisoned us?" he asked.

"Helen. What can I say—she's a witch from hell. She ground up glass into a fine powder and put it in the hamburgers we ate yesterday evening. There's nothing the doctors here can do for us. There's no reason for us to stay here. But Helen's not done. She's at the dock now with Pascal. No, I'm sure they've already set out. She's forcing him to take her to Delos. There she intends to kill him."

Tom frowned. "Isn't this a bit farfetched, Josie?"

"Look at the way you feel!" I shouted, before lowering my voice. "You have to trust me on this, Tom. There's no help for us here. All we can do now is save Pascal. She has to be stopped."

"But why would she drag him all the way to Delos to kill him? She could kill him here if she wished."

I wasn't about to try to explain the whole story to him. "She's lost her mind. She thinks she's some kind of goddess, and that she has to make a human sacrifice to one of the Furies—Alecto."

"I thought you were the one having the weird experiences."

"I was just having a few dreams. Helen's got a full-blown psychosis going. Tom, I can't argue with you about this anymore, there isn't time. You said yourself you have never been sick like this before. You haven't because you've never swallowed ground glass before. Understand these two points clearly—Helen did this to you, and she is going to do worse to your friend." I grabbed his arm. "We must leave here now before the others come to take us to Athens. Get up!"

Tom got up, much to my surprise. I'd had serious doubts about convincing him to accompany me to Delos. He put his shoes on and we opened the window beside his bed and climbed out into a row of bushes. It was all I could do to keep from screaming—every move seemed to rattle the glass inside me over raw nerve. Yet there's nothing like the desire for vengeance to drive one on, and it doesn't matter if the individual is mortal or immortal. I was going to drop dead before I let Phthia get away with her plan.

My motor scooter was parked in back of the health center. When Pascal and I brought Tom in, I had decided at the last second to go on my bike rather than in the truck. I had thought—correctly, I saw now— that I might need my bike for reasons unexpected. Pulling my keys from the pocket of my windbreaker, I got Tom on the back and started the bike with a hard kick, one that made me grimace. I peeled away from the miniature hospital.

When we were racing to the harbor, I called back over my shoulder, "I assume Pascal has already taken the motorboat that belongs to his boss. Do you know where we can get another?"

"We can steal one," Tom said.

"It's that easy?"

"Yes. Few people steal anything on Mykonos. So few people lock anything. But if Helen is as dangerous as you say, maybe we should first get the gun at my apartment."

"You have a gun? You just told me how peaceful Mykonos is. Why do you have a gun?"

"Pascal was having trouble with a man in town. That's how I met him—when he was in the middle of a fight with the guy."

"He told me. The man pulled a knife on him and you suddenly appeared and kicked it out of the man's hand. Then Pascal broke the guy's nose."

"Hardly. The guy raised a rolling pin to Pascal,

191

which I kicked out of the guy's hand, and then *I* hit the guy in the nose. Pascal is big and kind but a baby when it comes to violence. In a fearful moment he bought the gun for protection. He's never used it. I think he's forgotten he owns it."

I drove to the apartment. Tom was too weak to climb the stairs, so it was up to me to get the gun. I wondered how we were going to manage to scale Kythnos to rescue the Frenchman.

I found the gun, a small-caliber automatic, where Tom said it would be—in the bottom of Pascal's chest of drawers. I checked to make sure it was loaded, and found the clip full, but didn't search for more ammunition. Stuffing it in my belt under my windbreaker, I hurried back to Tom. Zeus had his thunderbolt— Josie her Smith & Wesson.

We circled the crowded portion of town and made it down to the dock by a back road. Several inflated dinghies lay pulled up on the sandy beach. Tom indicated we had our choice. Together we pulled one of the small boats into the water. Tom started the motor. His shot was already beginning to wear off. He was more alert, but also in more pain.

I had assumed Tom would steal a sailboat, since we didn't have keys for the motorboats. But he said he could hotwire any older boat that didn't have an elaborate locking mechanism. He pointed out that there was no wind, and that a sailboat would take a long time to reach Delos. It was true. The *meltémi* was resting, and I had never seen the night air so still. The moon was completely full, almost straight overhead.

Tom steered the dinghy up beside a powerful-looking but slightly worn motorboat. He climbed aboard first, clumsily, and almost ended up in the water. He had to help me onto the boat. As he bent under the steering wheel and tugged on the wires, I asked him if he paid for his tuition at Oxford by stealing cars.

"My father is a mechanic," he said. "He taught me everything he knows." He added, "When he was young he stole cars."

"Did he ever get caught?"

"He spent ten years in jail."

"That's a pity," I said.

Tom's eyes were on me, the moonlight bright on his pale face. He appeared to be a marble statue then. This was the first time I had studied him with the awareness of who I was, the first time the immortal had stared at the mortal. My love for him then was so great, his next question stung me as much as my bodily agony.

"How long will we be in this prison, Josie?" he asked.

He was referring to our pain. "It shouldn't last too long."

He nodded sadly. "We're goners, aren't we?"

I reached over and touched his arm. "There's still hope."

"How can we hope if what you say is true?" A spasm of pain shook him as if to remind him there was no denying the truth of my words. "No one can remove the glass from our bodies." He nodded. "We're going to die."

"So we die," I said. "So what? I know there is life beyond the grave. No, this is not a religious sentiment of mine, Tom. It is what I know. There is a heaven, there are many heavens. If we die, we will go to one of them together."

Such was the power of my words then, it was almost as if the goddess inside spoke through me. Tom was visibly moved. He nodded in what I believed was acceptance and returned to the wires.

A minute later the motor roared to life, and we were off.

The water was liquid glass. We plowed across the sea at high speed, neither of us breathing well, Tom worse off than me. His morphine was wearing off quickly, and halfway to Delos he asked me to take the wheel and sat down, balled up in pain. I was the one with the gun, the sure knowledge of what Helen could and would do. I wondered if I should put Tom through the strain of climbing Kythnos. It didn't seem logical. Yet I felt he should be with me. . . .

I don't know what I expected to happen on Kythnos to help Tom. Certainly lightning was not going to strike. The thunderbolts had left with Zeus, when he had gone off to God only knew which region. The best I could hope for was that we'd die in each other's arms—after we had stopped Helen.

How did I intend to stop her?

Was I prepared to kill her?

Yes.

I wanted to come upon Helen with as much stealth as possible. Although it added time, I circled around the north end of Delos, before bringing the boat to shore on the west side of Kythnos. I was almost certain Helen would have docked her boat on the east side of the pinnacle, since that would have brought her as close as possible to her objective. But with my choice of landing site, I had not added greatly to how far we had to walk—maybe two hundred yards at most.

We climbed out of the boat and started for Kythnos, picking our way through a few of the more obscure ruins of Delos. Surprisingly, I was not anxious to run into the island's security force. It could have been argued that we could use the police to stop Helen from harming Pascal. But my objective was to stop Helen permanently. No jail could hold her now that she was awakening to her true nature. Deep inside, her origin was demonic. She would cause the world untold suffering if she was left alive. I planned to put a bullet in her brain straightaway.

We reached the base of Kythnos less than ten minutes after leaving the boat. The pinnacle rose above us like a man-made silver cone. The island was silent as a tomb. The moon shone straight overhead like the Cyclop's eye burning a hole in the firmament. I remembered how hard it had been to climb the steps, but now we couldn't even use them, for Helen would see us approaching. We had to go up the west side of the hill, through the weeds, clinging to stones and gravel. After I pointed this out to Tom, he groaned, and fell to his knees.

"I don't know if I can make it, Josie," he whispered.

I helped him up and almost passed out from my own pain. "Think how beautiful the view will be from the top. Think how surprised Helen will be to see us."

Tom tried to smile. "Can we offer her a hamburger?"

I hadn't told him I was going to kill her on sight.

"We will offer her dessert," I said.

We started up. Five minutes into the climb I thought it was hopeless. We were both too weak. The last of my strength was evaporating in the brilliant moonlight. The sun would have been hotter and would have sapped my energy quicker. Yet I wished it had been in the sky instead of the moon. For the sun was the home of Apollo, and we were so near his birthplace. I pictured him on his throne on Mt. Olympus, so silent, so powerful, so all knowing.

Yet, at my trial, he had let me be condemned.

Why? I still didn't understand.

But the mere thought of him gave me a boost of energy. I pulled on Tom. "We're almost there," I whispered.

In reality we had to stop to rest three more times before we reached the summit. Our last break was very near the top, maybe fifty feet short of our goal. We clung precariously to the side, sharp stones digging into our ribs.

Our journey had not been in vain.

Above us, I could hear Helen and Pascal talking. But I couldn't hear what they were saying.

"What's the plan?" Tom whispered.

"I want you to stay here," I said. "I'll go up alone."

"But you dragged me up here so I could be with you when you confronted her."

"I brought you here for other reasons," I said simply. "You rest here for a moment." I removed the gun from my belt. "I'll call for you in a minute."

He grabbed my arm. "What are you going to do, Josie?"

I smiled. "Reason with her." I leaned over and gave him a quick kiss on his dusty cheek. "Don't worry, Tom, I won't be long."

He gave me a distrustful look but didn't argue.

I scrambled up the remainder of the hill to a large marble block that lay at the edge of the summit and that helped prevent tourists from falling off Kythnos. It was my initial intention to pause at the stone, maybe listen to Helen and Pascal for a moment to get a bearing on what was happening, before bolting onto the scene. As I listened, however, I heard nothing. I suspected Helen had noted our arrival. If that was the case, the situation would not improve with my waiting.

I jumped up onto the marble stone, my gun drawn. Helen and Pascal stood near each other in the center of the ring of stones that made up the secondary mount of the summit. The stones were low, useless for cover. It seemed I had not taken them by complete surprise; they were scanning the four directions when I appeared. Also, Helen did not freeze at my appearance. She saw the gun and quickly jumped behind Pascal.

"She has a gun," Helen said to Pascal. "She intends to shoot me."

Obviously the sacrifice to Alecto had not reached even the beginning stages. Pascal still seemed to be on good terms with Helen. But then I noticed a heaviness in the way he moved, as if he were slightly drugged. Of course, I knew as soon as I awoke from my final dream that Helen was capable of controlling him by the sheer force of her will. All demons, to varying extents, could dominate the will of an average human being. On Mt. Olympus, the practice was referred to as Seedling. Pascal was a nice guy, but no warrior. Tom, on the other hand, must have had tremendous internal strength. He had already resisted Helen's use of Seedling, as demonstrated by the fact that he had said no to her advances. Seedling was always connected to the use of sexuality—the perversion of it.

Pascal's expression was quizzical. "What are you doing, Josie?"

"Just out for a bit of fresh air," I said. "Let me talk to Helen for a minute, please."

"She's lying," Helen said, staying behind Pascal. "She intends to kill me."

"Josie, give me the gun," Pascal said, holding out his hand.

I climbed down from the stone, moving closer to them. "Pascal," I said. "You know how Tom and I are sick? It's because Helen poisoned us. You're shielding a very bad person. You can't imagine how bad. Step aside and let me take care of her."

"She's crazy," Helen said, fear entering her voice. "You can see how crazy she is, Pascal. Don't let her shoot me."

Pascal shook his hand. "Give me the gun, Josie. You don't want to hurt anyone."

"That's true," I said, being careful not to stumble on the broken pillars at my feet. "I don't want to hurt her." I raised the gun, aiming at Pascal's right hamstring. I was willing to wound him to get a clean shot at the witch. "I just want to blow her goddamn brains out!"

I pulled the trigger. The gun did not fire.

Then there was a hand on my arm, come from behind, pulling down my aim.

"No, Tom!" I cried.

"Get the gun, Pascal!" Helen shouted.

Tom was already on me, and Pascal didn't take long to reach me. A scuffle ensued, a confusion of struggling limbs and bitter cursing. The outcome was certain before the fight began. Tom and I were dying. Our strength was all but spent. Pascal, although slowed by the pressure of Seedling on his will, was still an easy match for both of us.

When the fight was done, Pascal had the gun.

He backed away from us, the weapon leveled at me.

Tom and I helped each other to stand.

"Dammit, Tom," I said bitterly.

"Pascal, don't give her the gun," Tom called.

Helen, suddenly standing tall and proud, chuckled. "Give me the gun, Pascal," she said.

"No!" Tom yelled.

Pascal handed the gun to Helen.

"See what I mean?" I grumbled. "She's a witch."

"Pascal, she's the one who poisoned us," Tom complained.

Helen toyed with the gun, as if it were a weapon too primitive for her lofty standards. "What nasty things has Josie said about me?" she asked. "Did she tell you that she tried to humiliate me before the assembly of gods?"

"I thought it best to leave out the Mt. Olympus parts," I said.

Helen chuckled. "I understand. What are you both worried about? You're both already dead. How do you feel, Tom?"

"Bitch," Tom swore.

Helen's grin was sly. She gestured to the sea that surrounded the island. "You didn't think that last summer when you swam naked with me in the ocean beneath the moonlight."

"You didn't tell me about that," I muttered to Tom.

Pascal stared at Helen, his face awash with innocence. "What are you doing with the gun?" he asked.

Helen was intrigued by the question and touched Pascal's face with her free hand, stroking his hair. He stood entranced with pleasure. It was her eyes that held the real power over him.

"I'm going to give you the gun," she said to him

slowly. "I want you to take it and put it in your mouth, Pascal. I want you to kiss it, and pretend you are kissing me." She handed him the gun. "Do it!" she hissed.

"No!" Tom cried.

Pascal smiled and took the gun and put it in his mouth.

"Touch the trigger," Helen whispered. "Touch it and pretend you are touching me, Pascal."

Pascal put two of the fingers of his right hand on the trigger. The act seemed to bring him sensual joy. He licked the end of the barrel. I would have closed my eyes, if my eyes in another life had not witnessed atrocities equally as great. Yet to watch the tragedy take place through mortal vision was particularly hard. Tom trembled by my side. He could not believe what was happening. He moved to intervene, but I stopped him. We were too feeble, and Helen could have taken us both easily. More important, he would not reach Pascal in time. He would only make himself an easy victim for her play. Helen glanced at me before she performed the next step in her sacrifice.

"Do you think my father would be pleased?" she asked me.

"I think you and your father need counseling," I said.

Helen snorted. "Squeeze me, Pascal. Squeeze the trigger."

Pascal squeezed the trigger.

The gun did not go off.

When I had used the gun a moment ago, it had also

failed to fire. I understood in a moment what the problem was—the safety was still on. I had failed to release it because the only experience I had had with guns was with my father's, a .22 Ruger, which was ready to fire when the safety switch was up. Apparently on a Smith & Wesson, the gun was only live when the safety was down. Pascal still had the switch up. Tom had told me his friend had never used the thing.

"Pascal!" I called, seeing an opportunity to break his trance. "You almost shot yourself in the mouth. Look at what you are doing!"

Pascal heard me. He pulled the gun from his mouth and gave it the most intense look I have ever seen a mortal give anything. His eyes turned as round as silver dollars. He sucked in a breath. Then his eyes rolled back and he collapsed to the ground. He had fainted; Tom had said he had a soft side. The gun bounced out of his hand, in our direction, and fell under a flat marble square.

Helen didn't leap for the gun. I could understand her reasoning. It had gone under a large rock and she would have to go down on her hands and knees to retrieve it. Also, she probably thought the thing was broken. It hadn't gone off in Pascal's mouth when he had pulled the trigger.

Plus she had another surprise up her sleeve.

Keeping her attention focused on us, Helen withdrew a long knife from her back pocket. Demons liked to cut mortals with knives, I knew, because then the mortal bled a lot. She walked toward us, the steel blade a sliver of evil light in her hand.

"I think it's time to get serious," she said.

"I feel the same way," I replied, jumping in front of Tom, who had fallen to his knees, exhausted. Tom struggled to get up as the witch raised the knife over her head, ready to stab down, but he was too weak. I was a poor bodyguard for him. Helen moved slowly closer, then sprang all at once. I lashed out at her with my right foot. The blow caught her in the shin, but it had little force behind it. Helen just laughed and kicked back at me. I dropped to the ground and rolled on my side. Helen towered over me, the moon glowing behind her head like an insane halo. She regarded me contemptuously.

"This is the end of our ancient rivalry, Josie," she said.

I crawled over the uneven ground at her feet. I was in such agony I almost wanted the end to come. But "almost" is a long way from throwing in the towel, at least for me.

"I thought we were just getting warmed up," I gasped.

Helen smiled without amusement. "The famous mouth, with all the right words. Tell me what you think about this." She raised her right leg. Too late I saw that my left shin was lying across the space between two hard stones. Helen stomped down with strength beyond most mortals. She was using powers I was unaware of. Not that it mattered. My mind was suddenly drowned by the awareness of my leg bone as it snapped under her pounding. I let out a scream, although I hated to give her the pleasure, and writhed on the ground at her feet. She knelt beside me and grabbed me by the hair, yanking my head back, exposing my throat. The knife gleamed in her free hand.

"I don't want you to leave just yet, Josie girl," she said. "I want you to enjoy what I am going to do to your lover. Then you can go to hell with an appetite for what you will receive there." She raised the knife again, threatening me. "Do you promise not to stray while I complete my little sacrifice?"

It was not the time for a smart-ass remark, I realized.

My vision was already swimming down into darkness.

So much pain, so much grief.

All because of one story that I told long ago.

"I promise, Phthia," I said.

She released me. "Good."

Helen stepped toward Tom, who was so close to death it should hardly have mattered what she did to him. But it mattered to me because I understood the extent of her cruelty. Because I had stared a Fury in the eye, and saw how black the heart of the devil could be. But my leg was broken, and I couldn't move. Helen reached down and pulled Tom to his feet, placing the knife at his throat. I glanced at Pascal, unconscious ten feet off to my right. He would not be coming to our rescue any time soon, I thought.

Helen dragged Tom to the south end of the summit of Kythnos. He put up feeble resistance. The south side was almost a sheer drop. She wasn't going to just push him off the side, I knew—that would have been too painless. She was going to make him bleed first.

I needed to get the gun. But I didn't know where it was exactly. The stone slab it slid under was six feet long. The moon was bright, but the shadow beneath the slab was deep. I realized I would have to spend several minutes on my belly feeling for the gun. No wonder Helen was unconcerned about it. I glanced over my shoulder. She had Tom at the precipice, holding him up as if he were a straw scarecrow before a flaming torch. She mocked him.

"No," I whispered.

I had to stop her.

There must be something I could use to stop her.

These thoughts were prayers.

I prayed for a miracle to happen as it had before when I was battered on the stormy sea.

A desperate idea came to me.

Desperate because I knew it would only postpone the inevitable a minute, if that long.

My camera was in the pocket of my windbreaker. It had a powerful flash attached to it. The light might startle Helen, bring her back after me. If I was fortunate, if I had the luck of a million mortals combined, perhaps she would stumble over the edge and die.

But that was not going to happen.

Still, I unzipped my pocket and pulled the camera free. It was a new model and threw a red beam on the subject before taking the picture. I focused through the lens on Helen. She was raising her knife to stab

Tom. My red light touched her head like an accusing finger.

I pressed the button. The flash went off.

Such a flash the world had never seen.

Suddenly the light of the midday sun exploded over Delos.

Kythnos could have been struck by a meteor of solar origin.

We were blinded, all of us, none more so than Helen, who never could take the sun. She staggered away from Tom, dropping her knife.

But she didn't stagger over the edge.

I didn't know the source of the light, but as swiftly as it came it began to fade, as if it were atomic in nature, and the fusion of atoms above our heads was now complete. In the dying yellow glow, I turned once more toward the slab. Now I could see the gun clearly, wedged beneath the stone in the corner closest to me. I crawled toward it and my fingers closed on the butt of the weapon just as the flare died completely and the moon once more reigned. But how weak the moonlight now seemed, with our eyes so startled. Nevertheless, I could see enough to find Helen. I removed the safety from the pistol and scampered to my knees, my broken calf howling in pain.

"Phthia!" I shouted. "I want to hear your story. The one you were going to tell the gods the day of the contest."

Helen stopped her staggering to look at me. With each passing second her form assumed more definition, a shadow across the black outline of the night. I wanted her to speak, to hear her words so that I could use them to sharpen my aim. Close by me, Pascal stirred.

"It was a story about your adultery," Helen said.

"I thought so," I replied.

I shot her, six times, in the chest. Each bullet pushed her back a step. She seemed surprised as the lead tore through her mortal flesh. The last bullet pushed her off the edge. She didn't scream as she fell. I believed her soul was already in hell before her body hit the ground.

I dropped the gun and lay down and closed my eyes.

It was my turn to die—to sleep, to forget for a while.

I don't know exactly how much time passed. When I opened my eyes next, Tom and Pascal were by my side. Pascal was crying. Tom had tears on his face as well. He touched my head, running his fingers through my blond hair. Yes, the hair of the blond girl, I thought, the daughter of the writer. In heaven, during the trial, I had watched the images and thought how fine the young mortal was—for a mortal. Now I knew she had been divine before I entered her body. Her life was a gift from God to the world. But now it had to end.

There was blood in my hair. My blood.

It reminded me of the blood in the statue.

How foolish that I had not realized before what it was.

My blood. My *immortal* blood.

A great god had left it for me to drink.

"Is it over, Josie?" Tom asked wearily.

"Not yet," I said. Using the last of my strength, I pulled the crystal statue of Sryope from my pocket. There was a slight indentation near the neck that I had not noticed before; it probably hadn't been there until now. The boys followed as I pressed the indentation with my finger and the head of the statue came off. Yet not a drop of the precious red fluid spilled. It was all in the body of the goddess.

"This is my blood," I whispered.

"Josie?" Tom asked.

"I want you to drink this," I said.

"What is it?" he asked.

"Wine," I said.

"The blessed wine," Pascal said suddenly.

I nodded and held the glass close to Tom's lips. "Drink and be well," I said.

He was watching me. "You drink it."

I laughed softly. "You're not afraid, are you?"

"Only for you," he said.

Somehow he understood what I was offering him. Maybe he was my old love, Aeneas. Maybe when Tom had been in his bicycle accident, the soul of my husband had entered his body, coming to Earth to find me. It was a possibility. All I knew for sure was that my love for him was a wonderful thing.

"Close your eyes and drink," I said. "There is only enough for one."

"It was meant for you," he protested.

"It was meant for love," I said. A tear ran over my

cheek. "Please drink so that I can see you well before I leave. You know I will not take it."

Tom hesitated, then nodded. He let me feed him the elixir. When he was through and the blood was gone, the statue fell from my hand and shattered like thin glass on the hard stones of Kythnos. Tom inhaled a deep breath and let out a sigh.

"The pain is gone," he said.

I nodded weakly. "It will never return. Your life will be rich and long."

"Josie," Tom cried, aware then that I was leaving.

My eyes closed. I wished to touch his face once more, but I couldn't move. "Think of me sometimes," I whispered. "I will think of you."

Tom's arms went around me. I could hear Pascal's tears. Neither could hold me in my body. My days on Earth were finished.

For now.

EPILOGUE

APOLLO STOOD BESIDE ME ON THE SUMMIT OF KYTHNOS. Dawn was coming. My body was gone, as were Tom and Pascal, although I don't believe they had been long gone. My blood still stained the holy stones. The ruins of Delos, spread out beneath our feet, seemed somehow lonely in the pale light.

"Were you really born here?" I asked Apollo. I had on the white robe of Sryope and was once more clothed in her radiant form.

"I was born before the Earth," Apollo said. "But I first set foot upon this world on this spot. For that reason, it is sacred."

"Did you send the flash of sunlight to save us from Phthia?"

"Yes. But you saved yourself."

"Who is my father?"

"You know."

211

"You're my father."

"Yes."

I was glad, but still confused. "Why didn't you defend me at the trial?"

He answered my question with a question. "What is wrong with paradise, Sryope?"

I thought of the gods of Mt. Olympus and many wrongs came to my mind: the sloth, the jealousy, the pettiness. But one problem was at the root of them all.

"No one grows there," I said.

Apollo nodded. "You are my daughter. I wanted the best for you. But you were a proud muse. You would never have entered the kingdom of mortals willingly."

"That's why you allowed me to be punished?"

"Was it such a great punishment? Or was it a great opportunity?"

I thought of all I had learned in the last year. "I understand."

Apollo continued. "Olympus is one door through which to enter the human kingdom. There are others. But once you pass through the human kingdom, and master what there is to learn there, you can go anywhere." He smiled at me. "This is the way the old ones went."

I was delighted. "Zeus and Athena became mortal?"

"Yes."

"Have I mastered all the ways of mortals?"

"No."

I was not disappointed. "That means I will have to return one day?"

"Yes. Next time you might even be born in a proper manner." He stopped and took my hand. His touch was warm as mortal skin. I believed he had been human many times, he knew so much. "But not today, Sryope. Today you go with me to my secret home in the sun. It is far above Mt. Olympus. I'm in need of a good story. Come, the way is long and the day has already begun."

"I don't have to stand before Minos and be judged?"

"No. The only mortals he gets a chance to judge are the ones who think they need it."

I laughed. "I thought as much." I tightened my grip on his hand as we prepared to leave Delos, adding, "I do have a story to tell. It starts with this girl on a plane."

Look for Christopher Pike's

The Wicked Heart

■ For the millions of late night television viewers of *The Jack Paar Show*, happily accustomed to going to bed with Jack Paar, this book fills an urgent need.

■ Left bereft when Jack abandoned his midnight talkathon for a weekly program, the abandoned insomniacs, who took Jack as a sleeping pill and found themselves hooked on benzedrine, can now go to bed with him again—although in a somewhat different form. Although they can no longer view him every weeknight from a horizontal position on their bedroom TV sets, they can now curl up with Jack in book form.

■ Here between soft covers, and convenient to be read there, are all the highlights of Jack's colorful five years of fun, feuds and frustrations. In *My Saber Is Bent* he recalls with typical candor and wit his travels and travails including his bullfight in Spain, his feud with Ed Sullivan and his renowned Berlin border incident.

MY SABER IS BENT was originally published by Trident Press-Simon and Schuster, Inc., at $3.95.

Also by Jack Paar

I KID YOU NOT

Published in a GIANT CARDINAL edition.